Swallowcliffe Hall

Eugenie's Story
1893

Books by Jennie Walters:

The Swallowcliffe Hall *series:*

Downstairs:
Polly's Story, 1890
Grace's Story, 1914
Isobel's Story, 1939
Upstairs:
Eugenie's Story, 1893

For teens:
See You in my Dreams

www.jenniewalters.com

Swallowcliffe Hall

Eugenie's Story

1893

Jennie Walters

Half Moon Press
London

Author's Note

Special thanks to Amanda Lillywhite for her invaluable help with both the content and the design of this book.

Whilst we have tried to ensure the accuracy of this book, the
author cannot be held responsible for any errors or omissions found therein. All rights reserved.

Copyright © Jennie Walters, 2007, 2011
Cover design by Amanda Lillywhite, *www.crazypanda.com*
Photograph of Victorian woman from the website of State University College, Oneonta, NY, with thanks,
 http://fash224.tripod.com/1890.html
Other cover photographs copyright © Jennie Walters, 2011
ISBN-10: 1492143995
ISBN-13: 978-1492143994

Swallowcliffe Hall, 1893

Thursday, February 23rd

What a day of ups and downs! It feels as though I've been shown a vision of Paradise, only to have the gates slammed shut in my face. After so many months in mourning, finally a chance to turn towards the sun, to welcome beauty and joy back into my life. And yet my stepmother seems determined to thwart me. What can I have done to deserve such cruel treatment? For lack of any other confidante, I've decided to keep a note of my trials and tribulations in this journal so that in happier times – which one day must surely come – I can look back and remember the storms of my youth.

The first inkling of disaster came yesterday. Mama summoned me to her room before dinner: a request that filled me with vague foreboding, though I had no idea what was to follow. She acknowledged the tragedy that had befallen me early in life before saying now it was time to look to the future; after careful deliberation, she and Papa had decided I might enjoy a visit to stay with my cousin in India. 'Connie sounded so much happier in her last letter,' she added, insincerely.

'India?' I repeated, momentarily thrown. It took a few seconds for the full meaning of her words to sink in. Have I become the kind of girl who needs to be packed off there to find a husband? Eugenie Vye, generally admitted to be the prettiest debutante of the 1890 season? With hair I can sit on, and a seventeen-inch waist? I couldn't restrain my outrage at the unfairness of the plan and jumped to my feet. 'You can't send me there! I simply won't go.'

'You will do as you're told,' came the icy reply. 'And this hysterical response shows why such a trip is necessary in the first place.' She leaned forward, grasping me by the wrist. 'In a couple of weeks you will be twenty-two. Time is passing, my dear – you need to play your cards with care.'

As if she needed to tell me that! Yet her iron grip only emphasized my vulnerability. 'But India is so unhealthy at this time of year,' I said, struggling to speak calmly. 'And the London season is about to begin.'

'I suppose you needn't leave straight away,' she said, dropping my hand to beckon Agnes over with her jewellery case. 'It will take a few weeks to arrange the details anyway. September might be a better time, when the rains are over and it's not so hot.'

'Yes, Mama,' I replied dully. Returning to my room as if in a trance, I sat at the dressing table to await Bessie's ministrations. Girls who go off to

Eugenie's Story

India come back leathery and shrunken, like a piece of old shoe leather – if they come back at all. The climate is too ghastly for words, Connie says, and ruins one's complexion for good. I refuse to believe poor Connie's happy; she's only putting on a brave face so her family won't worry. *She* is fortunate enough to have a mother who cares about her. This trip is all Mama's idea, I'm sure of it; only someone outside the family who didn't truly love me would dream of sending me away. Tears prickled at my eyes. Imagine the shame of it! Bessie looked at me pityingly which caused her to poke my scalp with a hairpin. She really is the clumsiest creature; I had to slap her hand to encourage her to concentrate.

By the time my toilette was finished, I had managed to rally a little. I have at least won a stay of execution, and surely by September I will have attracted a number of proposals from which to choose. In my first season, I had fifteen or more – most of them easy enough to turn down. Darling Freddie was different from the start. He told me he had fallen in love with the nape of my neck as I played the piano that summer evening in the drawing room at St James's Square. I remember turning around to see his gaze upon me and smiling back, because he was so handsome and tall and charming, and I had already begun to have feelings for him myself: a sort of queer fluttering leap in my stomach whenever I saw him, or thought of him, or even were his name to be mentioned in company. I found myself blushing when he spoke to me, and the witty remarks that usually came so readily died on my lips. Not that it seemed to matter. We could communicate without speaking because our hearts were open to each other. I knew he would ask me to marry him, and I knew what I would reply when he did. The excitement of getting engaged in one's first season! He was twenty-five, the son of the Earl of Brixham, and everything I could possibly have hoped for. It is heartbreaking to think he has already been dead twice as long as the entire period of our courtship. Is he to remain the love of my life? Will I ever find another to take his place?

Yet Mama is right in one respect at least: the past is over and now I must turn my energies towards the future. Admittedly I am no longer the young ingénue but perhaps I have other qualities to offer – a certain sophistication, the ability to make light-hearted conversation, an understanding of fashionable society. (And those long hours spent on the piano or busy with my embroidery must count for something.) I am worldly enough to know such assets are not sufficient, however; I need more tangible weapons in my armoury. A fashionable wardrobe is one of them. I have always admired my sister-in-law's taste, so when Kate told Mama and me a few weeks ago she had discovered a wonderful dressmaker who came highly recommended by many of her friends, and asked if we would like to visit her too, I readily agreed. Kate is one of those rich American girls who seem to be everywhere in society nowadays, yet she prefers to buy her gowns in London rather than Paris and always manages to look attractive. In my opinion she could take a little more trouble over her hair, but she seems happy with her maid so I have refrained from commenting – discretion being the better part of valour.

*

We left Swallowcliffe in good time this morning for our appointment with Mrs Thompson, the *modiste*: my stepmother, Kate and I, plus Agnes, to carry parcels and help with buttons. Agnes has been Mama's maid for years and is becoming something of a problem, getting in a muddle and forgetting things. Frankly it would have been more useful to bring Bessie but that would have caused terrible ructions in the servants' hall and poor Agnes wouldn't have been able to hold her head up there again. Thomas took us to the railway station in the brougham, from where we were to catch the London train. I still felt a little raw from my encounter with Mama the previous evening but worse was to follow. While we were waiting on the platform, she announced casually, 'Your father's generosity has its limits, Eugenie. Your dress allowance must remain at fifty guineas this year, so please bear that in mind. However I'm told Mrs

Thompson's prices are very reasonable.'

Taken completely by surprise, I was lost for words, and then the train drew in so we had all the fuss of finding our first-class carriage and dispatching Agnes to second, climbing aboard and settling down. I'm sure her timing was intentional. 'But, Mama,' I said, when at last I could speak, 'I've hardly spent anything on clothes for months! Surely you realize how important it is for me to be properly turned-out this season? Especially in the light of our discussion yesterday.'

She merely looked at me coldly and replied, 'Don't be impertinent. Your presentation gown and your mourning wardrobe were a considerable expense, and so is that new maid of yours. You must learn to cut your coat to suit your cloth.'

My presentation gown is nearly three years old, though, and as for my mourning wardrobe – I should like to set fire to every one of those hideous crape shrouds and warm my hands on the blaze! Has she any idea how wretched it has been for me to shuffle about in black, peering out at the world from behind my veil like some short-sighted crow? By now I'm even sick of the burgundy bombazine and grey poplin that seemed such a liberation six months ago. (My maid Bessie is a mixed blessing, too.) It would seem my stepmother has written off my prospects and decided to wash her hands of me. I can think of no other explanation for her

Eugenie's Story

unreasonable behaviour: telling me I haven't long to find a husband while deliberately limiting my chances of doing so. You might as well enter a horse for the steeplechase with its legs hobbled.

I spent the rest of the journey staring out of the window while trying to calculate how far fifty guineas would stretch, even with 'reasonable prices'. When the train arrived at Charing Cross station, Agnes finally managed to rejoin us (having left Mama's umbrella behind in the luggage rack) and we set about finding a growler to take us on to the dressmaker. Kate tried to lighten the atmosphere as the four of us sat silently in the carriage. 'I'm most intrigued to meet Mrs Thompson,' she said, squeezing my arm. 'Letty Morgan says her teagowns are exquisite.'

But I could not disguise my feelings and sat in a bitter fug of gloom as they talked about this brave little woman whose husband had run off with a chorus girl, leaving her with only his name and a child to support, and dressmaking her only chance of earning a living. She had set up shop in her mother's house and was selling gowns to her friends. Well, no wonder her prices were reasonable; so they should be. And Letty Morgan is hardly the last word in taste. You will gather I had no great hopes for the appointment, which seemed to accord with my stepmother's penny-pinching.

At last we arrived at an ordinary little house

in a road somewhere behind Oxford Street, to be welcomed by a maid (no cap) and shown into a front parlour crowded with upright chairs and bolts of material stacked against the wall. Agnes had to lurk in the hall outside. I could hear a child crying upstairs, then running footsteps heralded the arrival of a somewhat breathless Mrs Thompson. My first impression was of a presentable, youngish woman with brown hair and a pleasant expression. She welcomed us all before taking my stepmother into a back room for the first consultation. I sensed Kate's concern but denied myself the luxury of her sympathy and leafed through a copy of *Sporting Life* which was lying on a side table. My sister-in-law can have no conception of my predicament, with all her father's shipbroking dollars in the bank and Swallowcliffe to command when Edward inherits the title. She can afford to be magnanimous.

Eventually Mama returned, rather flushed in the face, and Kate was taken away for her turn. She's blessed with many natural assets: coppery hair, green eyes and a fresh complexion among them. She seems a little careworn these days – though what she has to worry about, I really can't imagine. The Dower House has been fitted out from attic to cellar according to the very latest specifications. There's electric light in every room, even the kitchen and the servants' hall, and no fewer than three of the bedrooms have been turned into bathrooms, with hot water constantly running out of the taps and emptying away down a drain! Goodness knows what the housemaids find to do all day, not having to carry water cans up and down stairs. In fact, she's in danger of spoiling the servants completely, always talking to them and asking how they are. She wants them to like her but it only confuses them to be treated so personally; they need clear boundaries or who knows what they'll get up to. When at last I'm mistress of my own household I shall lay down rules so that everyone from housekeeper to scullery maid can see exactly what is required of them. Fair but firm. I shudder to imagine what will happen at Swallowcliffe when Kate takes up the reins. Luckily my father is in excellent health so that won't be for a while, I hope, and perhaps in a few years she may have learnt a thing or two.

My stepmother and I exchanged not a word as we sat there, pretending to read magazines and listening to the occasional murmur from Mrs Thompson with answers from Kate in her casual drawl. I must admit, my curiosity was piqued. If I hadn't been so angry with Mama and if she hadn't been so naturally unforthcoming, I should have asked her what to expect. At one point she rose to finger a roll of sea-green chiffon propped against the wall with a light in her eye I'd never seen before: a sort of hungry greed, tempered with the prospect of imminent satisfaction. Like a lioness returning to the kill. How I wished I could have had my own dear mother with me, whose sweet face and gentle voice are slowly fading from my memory. She would have given me loving advice, having only my best interests at heart, and we could have consulted Mrs Thompson together. (There would have been no question of a fifty-guinea allowance, either.) But it's no use complaining. I must deal with the blows Fate has dealt me as best I can.

At last it was my turn to be shown into the inner sanctum: a small boudoir fitted out with a table, cheval mirror, chaise longue and dressmaker's dummy. The table was littered with pins, cotton reels, silk roses and ribbons; swathes of satin, velvet, chiffon and lace festooned the chaise and cascaded in a vibrant waterfall from the curtain rail to the floor. The whole room glowed with colour: from blush pink to the deepest crimson, from vivid indigo and vermilion through to palest eau-de-nil. We might have been standing in some exotic Bedouin tent. Agnes stifled a yawn behind her hand but if Mrs Thompson was tired from her previous appointment, she showed no sign of it; her eyes were bright and she seemed full of energy. 'My dear Miss Vye,' she said, taking my hands in hers, 'may I tell you a little about the way I work? Every one of my gowns is individual, inspired by the personality of the lady for whom it is designed. I should like to study you for a few moments, if I may, to see what will suit you best. We must be sure to do you justice. Your complexion is exquisite, and may I compliment you on your figure? I have to recommend a tighter lacing of the corset to some of my clientèle but in your case that would be quite unnecessary.'

I was taken aback by this, naturally – both the physical contact and the idea of being contemplated in this way – but already bewitched by that room and its presiding genius. I stood quietly while she flitted about like a busy little humming bird swooping on a flower: draping fabric against my body, taking measurements with the tape around her neck, even removing my hat to adjust my hair! From time to time she would stand back and look at me, her head on one side, but with such kindly interest that I basked in the attention.

'I think I have it,' she said eventually. 'At first I thought of presenting you as an innocent maiden, a naiad, all fresh-faced and dewy-eyed, but you have too much character for that. Your charm has been tempered by sorrow, forged into something altogether more remarkable. Those sad dark eyes of yours are quite bewitching. If I may say so, Miss Vye, you have the potential to become one of the leading beauties of your generation.'

This was too much. I sat down on the chaise longue and promptly burst into tears.

'My dear young lady!' Mrs Thompson exclaimed, perching beside me and clasping my hands again. 'Whatever is the matter?'

It was hard to explain that after so many months in the wilderness, such appreciation was enough to disarm me. After Mrs Thompson had sent Agnes off to fetch a cup of tea, I tried to tell her something of what happened to me last year. Her own eyes filled with sympathetic tears. 'You poor girl,' she murmured, offering me a handkerchief trimmed with lace and exquisitely embroidered forget-me-nots. 'How tragic! And you had been engaged less than a month? The trousseau not even begun?'

I shook my head, unable to speak. 'Never mind, Miss Vye,' she declared, patting my knee and springing to her feet. 'I shall help you find the happiness you deserve. In one of my gowns, you will be irresistible. In fact I can promise you another fiancé before the season's out.'

'But I only have fifty guineas!' I told her, blowing my nose. 'Barely enough for a teagown and something to wear to the theatre, let alone shoes or a wrap. What is to be done?'

She looked at me thoughtfully. 'Perhaps we should start with one day dress and a truly stunning gown for the evening, and see what happens. Some of my ladies have their bills settled by admirers, or I could always let you have a little something on account. Put yourself in my hands. And now, to work!'

There followed perhaps the most enjoyable

half hour of my life. Patiently, Mrs Thompson guided me towards the tones that would flatter my complexion and the cut that would make the most of my figure. (Thank goodness the fashion for bustles is over and the line is so much more fluid now.) She sketched out various details on a pad for me to approve: embroidery on a puffed gigot sleeve, or tiny silk rosebuds just visible beneath a filmy chiffon overskirt. These flowers are made individually by hand. The petals are cut from two shades of pink silk gauze and the wired stems are bound in different shades of green; each one is a miniature work of art. And the colours we chose! For the teagown, lavender chiffon over a dress of the palest blue brocade, scattered with rosebuds on the bodice and lavishly trimmed at the sleeves and neck with lace. In fact the lace is machine-made, but so skilfully that no one would ever know. There will be a cherry pink sash, pink silk buttons running down the back and a pink petticoat underneath trimmed with the same lace. My evening gown is to be made from white satin with a silver sash and embroidered overskirt and train, and a slightly lower *décolletage* than my presentation gown, although nothing too showy. Utterly ravishing, and she promises it will be ready for the Hunt Ball in just over a month's time.

Together, we were inspired. Mrs Thompson shook out a length of the glimmering satin and threw it over my shoulder, folding and gathering with her skilful fingers into an approximate shape. 'There,' she breathed, leaning back to admire her handiwork. 'You are radiant, Miss Vye.'

It was hard to disagree. Mrs Thompson may not yet be a grand couturier with an international reputation but she is a true artist. To think what I might become were she to design me a whole wardrobe, complete with underclothes and *peignoir*...

*

We sat quietly on the carriage-ride back to the railway station, the three of us preoccupied with our own visions of glory – or so I thought – and Agnes dozing surreptitiously in the corner. Yet when my stepmother roused herself to ask what frocks we had ordered, Kate seemed strangely unenthusiastic. Apparently Mrs Thompson is making her a pale green teagown, a tweed and velvet walking costume, a cotton morning dress and a gold velvet ballgown trimmed with pearls, antique lace and sprays of red roses. (She has two assistants but, even so, I hope she will have my order finished on time.)

'Of course it's lovely to have pretty clothes,' Kate went on, 'but I can't help feeling guilty about spending so much money. I went to see Mrs Beamish yesterday. She's just had her sixth child and her husband's at home with a broken leg. Think what a difference ten guineas would make to her life.'

'Very little at all, I should imagine,' Mama

retorted tartly. 'Mr Beamish would only spend it on drink and land her with another sickly baby to look after.' And she gave Agnes a jab with her elbow, to wake her up.

Quite. It occurred to me that Kate's been spending a lot of time recently visiting the poor, and this might be where the problem lies. Anyone would feel lack-lustre, listening to their endless tales of woe. Besides, as I told her, beautiful clothes bring almost as much pleasure to the beholder as to the person who wears them. Surely Mrs Beamish would rather open her door to a person feeling happy and looking perfectly lovely in the latest fashions than a frump in some dowdy outfit. Why, it's our duty to dress as well as we can when calling on the needy, to cheer them up. *Noblesse oblige*, after all...

Mrs Thompson has given me some hope for the future, despite Mama's lack of compassion and support. New vistas are opening up before me but the months ahead are crucial. I must plan my campaign for this season as carefully as any military commander, since it will probably determine the rest of my life. I cannot afford to defy my stepmother; she is too powerful and needs to be handled diplomatically if I am ever to blossom in my own right. Mrs Thompson is a significant arrow in my quiver. Who knows, perhaps she might help me turn my maid into another? Although Bessie still leaves a great deal to be desired, she is younger than Agnes and may be more malleable. She could learn some of Mrs Thompson's tricks of the trade, or even copy her designs — although that might be stretching her capabilities too far. As Nanny Roberts used to say, you can't make a silk purse out of a sow's ear.

Any hope is tempered with realism, however, for the prospect of falling in love again seems remote to me at the moment. There have been so many balls this past long winter that I should have enjoyed, despite the mourning trims on my gown, yet none of my partners managed to please me. Lord McGillie, the Earl of Tarbert's son, was most attentive but his compliments left me unmoved. He has gone to the Riviera for a few weeks so my feelings may have changed by the time I see him again, but I doubt it. Mrs Thompson is right: grief has had a profound effect on me. And Lord McGillie is rather short — the type of man, in fact, who runs to fat in middle age.

There is no point upsetting myself. I simply must find a way of geeing up Bessie and getting a few more gowns out of Mrs Thompson. Perhaps if I can talk to Papa on his own, he may agree to raise my allowance…

Eugenie's Story

Tuesday March 7th
A most heavenly house party at the Galbraiths'. Their home is so warm and comfortable. So many fires! One in my bedroom while dressing for dinner and in the morning, a housemaid was on her knees at the hearth when I awoke – without even having to ask. I'd brought Bessie with me, and it must have been an education for her to see how things are done at Shadwell. Mary and Maude are such fun. Maude is seventeen and looking forward to her first season; Mary a year and a half younger than I. Their sister Margaret, my contemporary, has married a young lion in the Tory party and is emerging as an accomplished hostess in her own right.

A huge ball and supper had been arranged for the Saturday night. I wore my presentation gown of ivory satin and white Chantilly lace, minus the full-length train of course, and felt only slightly handicapped by the fact it's three years old. Each guest drew a slip of paper with a name written on it from a hat (a topper for the gentlemen, a bonnet for the ladies) and looked for a partner with the matching half to be taken into dinner. We danced increasingly wildly till dawn. When word got out it was my birthday, I found myself serenaded by a succession of beaux. Managed only a couple of hours' sleep before a maid appeared with an invitation to breakfast in Mary's room with Lavinia, Maude and Barbara. Hot scones, crisp bacon and eggs cooked all manner of ways were brought on huge trays by the servants, to be consumed over a most enjoyable dissection of the evening before. Eventually Clem and Cynthia appeared from breakfast downstairs with news from the dining-room: apparently an unknown young man had been found asleep in the conservatory behind a potted palm and George Galbraith was still flirting outrageously with Sarah Fulbrooke even though she's been married less than a year. Dancing again on the Sunday but upstairs to bed shortly after midnight – only to steal out again with Mary and Lavinia for a night-time stroll round the gardens, wrapped in our eiderdowns.

We said our goodbyes on Monday, promising to meet again in London when the season is under way, and were taken to the station somewhat bleary-eyed. A minor crisis at Hardingbridge station as Bessie and the guard had managed to mislay my trunk. It was eventually found but the delay was excruciating when all I wanted was to curl up in my own bed. I was struck by the different atmosphere of my home from that of the Galbraiths'. Shadwell is a little faded around the edges and one usually has to turf a dog out of one's chair before sitting down, but it's full of laughter and conversation. Although Swallowcliffe is magnificent, Mama hasn't made it welcoming. She isn't naturally hospitable and that has implications for my prospects. Other mothers make a point of seeking out congenial company for

Eugenie's Story

their children, arranging house parties and picnics and other happy occasions at which young friends can mingle. Beyond an initial ball in my honour that first season, I have had to fend for myself, with only mad Aunt Georgina as a reluctant chaperone.

I am feeling tired today and out of spirits. A terrible vision has wormed its way inside my head. This is my nightmare: failing to find a suitor in England this season, I am dispatched to India, only to be unsuccessful there too and sent back to this country, wrinkled as a prune and hopelessly outdated, to live out the rest of my days at Swallowcliffe as Mama's increasingly embittered companion. In the clear light of day I can dismiss these fears as ridiculous but in the wee small hours, when it seems the night watchman and I are the only two people awake in the world, they seem only too believable, and I have to ring for Bessie to bring me a mug of hot milk before sleep will return.

Friday March 17th
Yesterday Mama asked to see me in her drawing-room. I was immediately anxious but she only wanted to tell me that Mrs Thompson's assistant would be arriving the next morning, bringing with her Kate's day dress and walking costume, the brocade evening cloak trimmed with sable for Mama, and my teagown. It has been arranged that she will stay with us at Swallowcliffe until Sunday, so she can make any adjustments required after a final fitting and help us to dress for dinner on the Saturday night, when we are entertaining guests. Apparently Mrs Thompson trusts her implicitly. Her name is Miss Veronica Pratt and I'm looking forward very much to her arrival.

'Miss Pratt may have some time to spare on the Saturday afternoon,' my stepmother said. 'Perhaps she could look through your wardrobe to see if anything can be done with your mourning frocks.'

Rather than dismiss her suggestion out of hand, I decided to thank her for letting me meet Mrs Thompson, and said how much I was looking forward to trying on my teagown. It was a wise approach, for Mama seemed to soften a little. At any rate, she unbent so far as to tell me about the guests for dinner on Saturday night. Of course Plum has been invited, as he is such an old friend of Mama's and an adornment to any social occasion; Swallowcliffe is practically his second home. His proper title is the Duke of Clarebourne but he has

Eugenie's Story

always been Plum to us, I'm not entirely sure why (perhaps because of his livery colours, which are purple and grey).

'Plum's bringing a friend with him,' she went on. 'A young Irishman, who is apparently quite charming and will even up the numbers. And Lady Duxford is coming with Charlotte and Henry; he can take you into dinner. Such a pleasant young man. I do hope you'll make an effort to be agreeable.'

Well of course I will, though Henry Duxford hardly cuts a dashing figure. When he talks I can't take my eyes off his Adam's apple, bobbing up and down, and he has the most unfortunate laugh. The family lives near by and we've known them for years. My feelings must have been written on my face because my stepmother said sharply, 'You could do a lot worse. Henry has delightful manners and he is an only son, after all.'

So this is her plan! But the only son of a baronet is hardly a great prize, and Duxford House is such an ugly red-brick mausoleum that the very sight of it looming on the horizon is enough to dampen one's spirits. I'd sooner live by myself in our gate lodge than be shut up there with the Duxfords en masse. Charlotte is pious and wispy, Lady Duxford never stops talking and Sir John is always off hunting big game abroad (probably as a result).

'Perhaps you would like to give the matter some thought.' Mama narrowed her eyes. 'I shall lend you my pearls tomorrow – wear them with your grey silk. And do try not to fidget. You must learn to cultivate an air of quiet assurance. How are your hands? Show them to me.'

As a matter of fact, my skin is in better condition than it has been for months. I've been wearing cotton gloves at night to prevent scratching when half-asleep, and Bessie has been making me a tisane of alder-root to drink and applying a poultice of potato flour to my hands every day. I couldn't bear to hold out for Mama's inspection like some naughty child, however, and rushed out of the room with a muttered excuse, angry tears prickling at my eyes. Sometimes it's impossible to act tactically, despite one's best endeavours.

The truth of the matter came in a blinding flash as I was dressing for luncheon. My stepmother is jealous of me. Of course! Although she knows it's her duty to help me marry well, she doesn't want me to eclipse her. That's why she won't intervene to secure me a reasonable clothing allowance, and why she wants to palm me off with Henry Duxford. She is probably struggling with the desire to be rid of me (which explains India) and the wish to keep me in her shadow here at home. The fact I'm Papa's favourite daughter because I look so like my mother is yet another factor counting against me. Well, I may still be vulnerable but at least now I understand the situation, I thought, contemplating my reflection with satisfaction as Bessie helped me into a velveteen skirt and pintucked blouse with cross-cut jabot. I shall have to put this understanding to good use...

Unfortunately Bessie is still proving a trial just when I need her most. I don't know what can be keeping her so busy but she is frequently hard to find and slow to answer my summons. The other day I had to ring the bell repeatedly, to discover in the end she had been closeted away in the laundry of all places. If only one felt there were a little more going on inside that vacant-looking head of hers! I suppose not everyone can be blessed with a quick intelligence but I doubt we shall ever come to much of an understanding – which is a pity, as she should be a welcome ally. Kate and her maid are thick as thieves, even though Hortense is French.

Kate had been invited for luncheon alone as my brother Edward had not yet returned from salmon-fishing in Scotland, and Harriet came down from the schoolroom to practise the art of conversation. She must surely be coming out next year, although she doesn't seem in much of a hurry, and she'd better have cultivated a few opinions by then. It hardly matters what you say so long as you say *something*, as I've told her many times. We discussed Oscar Wilde, whose book she has just finished, and the Royal Family: the Prince and Princess of Wales celebrated their thirtieth wedding anniversary last week, and the Queen is shortly leaving for Florence aboard the

Royal Yacht. We ate pork galantine followed by plum pudding, although I didn't have much of an appetite. The new footman dropped a fork.

Oddly enough, I noticed that Kate spent some time closeted with my father alone in the library when she first arrived, and that she seemed preoccupied during the meal. She wasn't even interested in the news that Mrs Thompson's assistant will be arriving with two of her frocks, although she is coming to dine at the house on Saturday night with Edward, who will have returned by then. When luncheon was finished, I asked whether I might walk back with her to the Dower House; she had come on foot because it was such glorious weather. I needed a breath of air to clear my head and, I must confess, I was curious to find out what she and Papa had been discussing.

When I had changed into a walking skirt, we set off around the back of the house past the stables and the carpenter's workshop. Kate had to stop and speak to everyone: the farrier, busy shoeing the carriage horses; the coachman, washing down our barouche; even the hallboy, absorbed in some mysterious task involving flowerpots. I began to think we would be standing there all afternoon, but it gave me time to reflect on the familiar world that is Swallowcliffe, my childhood home. I couldn't picture a similar scene in India, though Connie has been to a polo match so they must have horses and therefore men to look after them. What about carriages, though? I've seen photographs of ladies being transported by natives in a sort of litter, which looks most undignified and is surely impractical for long journeys.

At last we got away and walked along the edge of the park. The sun was shining, the oak trees were bursting into fresh green leaf and I could smell a tang of wild garlic on the breeze. Kate pointed out a couple of fawns among the fallow deer and in the nearby field, lambs were clustering by their mothers or skipping over the grass. Without warning, I became completely overwhelmed; Kate had to sit me down on a tree stump. She was so kind and sympathetic, I found myself telling her about India, although that wasn't the idea behind our walk at all. 'It won't come to that,' she reassured me, smoothing the hair off my face. 'Don't lose heart, dear! Not now, when there is everything still to play for.'

Of course she had once been in the same position as I, and not so very long ago. When I asked if she had found it easy to decide whether to marry Edward, she replied that no one can ever be sure beyond all doubt; the only thing for it is to take a leap into the dark with a stout heart and a sense of duty, and then make the best of one's decision – which didn't sound particularly romantic. It's certainly not how I felt when Freddie proposed. When I had recovered a little, she helped me to my feet and we walked slowly on until we had reached the road and the Dower House was within sight. She hesitated for a moment before taking my arm and turning the other way, towards the village. 'Come, let's make a detour,' she said mysteriously. 'I want to show you something.'

Stone Martin is an unexceptional place, consisting of a church, a public house, a pond, a collection of dreary labourers' cottages and not much else. I thought for one heart-sinking moment we might be calling on the Beamishes but thank goodness that wasn't it. Kate stopped outside a derelict barn on the outskirts of the village, half a mile or so from the Swallowcliffe gates. It was an unpromising sight: the roof had long since disappeared and a rusty sheet of corrugated iron was propped across the doorway. Well, it turns out she has plans for this eyesore. She has asked my father whether it can be knocked down for almshouses to be built in its place, to accommodate six elderly people! He is to provide the land and she, I discovered after some discreet questioning, will pay the building costs – which I should imagine will run into many hundreds or even thousands of pounds, no matter how simple the construction. 'Don't you think such houses are sorely needed?' she said. 'There's nowhere for destitute old folk in the parish, only the workhouse at Hardingbridge which is a God-forsaken place if ever I saw one.'

I told her a group of ladies from the town were working hard to improve conditions there but she dismissed this with a wave of her hand, saying it would be a hundred years before <u>they</u> got anything done. 'We could have a row of houses built by next summer, imagine that!' And she started talking about architects and carpenters, and the importance of drainage. When I asked her what Edward thought of the plan, however, she was non-committal.

It all seems most odd. Why has she spoken to my father before discussing this project with her husband? It's almost as though she waited until Edward had gone away to raise the matter when surely, he and my father should be the ones in charge of any building on the estate. I'm sorry to say so but the whole business smacks of self-glorification. Although I like Kate – very much – I can't help thinking that as the only child of wealthy and indulgent parents, she's grown too used to getting her own way. Surely it would be more tactful to work through channels that already exist, such as the Gentlewomen's League for Workhouse Improvement, rather than forging ahead on her own like a bull in a china shop. She would do well to bear in mind that she is, after all, a relative newcomer to these shores before she goes knocking down part of our heritage and rebuilding it as she thinks fit.

Her response to my cautiously-phrased objections was not reassuring. 'But I must have a project. Something worthwhile to do, beyond changing from one frock into another, playing bridge and gossiping.'

Of course she must! Her project is to make her husband happy, support him in all his endeavours and, without wishing to sound indelicate, carry on the family line. Edward and Kate have been married for nearly two years and she's still as slim as a reed. She ought to be resting and eating properly, not tramping round the village on unnecessary schemes. The elderly are perfectly all right where they are; practically every cottage one visits has a grey head nodding away in the corner. Still, it's not my place to offer an opinion. No doubt Edward will put his foot down when he returns from Scotland and that will be the end of that.

Saturday March 18th

The transformation of Bessie has begun! Part of the problem, I realized with one of those flashes of inspiration that seem to come so regularly to me now, is her name. 'Bessie' sounds positively bovine, and her surname is Cheesman which presents further difficulties. I can't go about calling 'Cheesman!' – it would be too ridiculous and has connotations with trade. I have decided to call her Beth, which is so much more refined. The name makes me think of *Little Women*, one of my favourite books, and while Bessie (as was) may never reach the fictional Beth's heights of saintliness, she has now been leant a certain dignity.

More to the point, however, Mrs Thompson's redoubtable assistant has helped me take her in hand. Miss Pratt arrived this morning on the London train with a quantity of trunks and hatboxes. She seems a practical young woman, rather lean and toothy but stylishly turned out in a tailored costume with a high-collared blouse and waistcoat, topped off by a natty straw boater. The effect was both smart and professional. Although she doesn't have Mrs Thompson's artistic vision (that would be too much to expect), she's clearly skilful and knows a great deal about fashion. I decided as soon as we met this morning that she would be a good influence on Beth, and so it has turned out. The three of us have spent all afternoon together – and most productively, too.

First I tried on the teagown, which is absolutely exquisite and very comfortable. (Mrs Thompson says one's corset doesn't need to be laced quite so tightly when wearing a flowing design, although I prefer to be well drawn-in at all times.) It's the most gorgeous confection of chiffon and lace, completed by the addition of a ravishing Botticelli flower wreath Miss Pratt had brought with her in case I wanted to borrow it for the evening. Yes, I most certainly did! I gazed at myself in the mirror, breathless with excitement, and even Beth was moved to offer some indistinct compliment. Miss Pratt showed her a charming new way to dress my hair, a little lower at the nape of the neck and loosely waved around clusters of artificial ringlets. It was quite a wrench to take off the dress after we'd made a couple of adjustments, but there was more work to be done. We looked through all the gowns in my wardrobe to decide which could be given away, which were to be stored in brown holland bags, and which could be made to last another year with the addition of a new collar, *fichu* or overskirt, or remodelling of the sleeves (so much fuller this spring).

Miss Pratt had all sorts of helpful suggestions, and I gather she and Beth are going to spend some time sewing together this evening while we are at dinner. This is exactly what the girl needs: wise advice from a fashionable but practical person who can show her by example how to behave.

Eugenie's Story

Miss Pratt manages to combine deference with a lively sensibility. I can't help wishing she were my maid, although no doubt Mrs Thompson would be reluctant to lose her. Still, Beth is already looking up. There's a certain spring in her step this evening and she's added a couple of unexpected touches to my toilette: a ribbon around my waist and a discreet dusting of powder over my *décolletage*.

Now I am sitting alone at the dressing table. Beth has gone to attend to Harriet and the maid has emptied my bath and put more coal on the fire. Around me, the house has swung into action with customary precision as preparations are made for the evening ahead; like the astronomical clock with its little moving figures we saw in Prague last year. Flowers have been cut from the hothouse for the decorator to arrange in vases and tureens, vegetables have been dug from the garden and washed in the scullery, wine and champagne have been brought from the cellar to the butler's pantry, the dining table is heavy with white damask, silver and crystal.

Mrs Bragg will be shouting at her skivvies over the noise and steam of the kitchen, Mr Goddard will be decanting the Château Lafitte in his pantry, the footmen will be powdering their hair, the housemaids doing whatever it is housemaids do that means they're always in the way *just* when one would like a little time to oneself. (Great news from the servants' hall: Perkins, an industrious creature, has just been promoted to head housemaid. Mrs Henderson seems to think highly of her and one can only hope her confidence is justified.) The first dressing gong has sounded. My father will be staring glumly at himself in the mirror while Steadman fusses around him, dreaming of dining alone in the library on hot buttered toast and Gentleman's Relish with the dogs at his feet. Agnes will be fastening my stepmother's jewels as Mama casts a final eye over the *placement*. Credit where it's due, she has a genius for seating arrangements. Next door, Plum will be enjoying a quiet glass of whisky in his customary room overlooking the rose garden. Further afield, a carriage will even now be clattering away from Duxford House. Inside it Lady Duxford will be haranguing her children, who are ignoring her as usual: Charlotte nervously adjusting her dress, wondering whether my brother Rory has been invited to dinner, and Henry staring into the dusk, hoping he is to sit next to me.

I am busy with plans of my own. The prospect of India has made me reckless. Mama's pearls lie before me in their unopened case and the grey silk gown still hangs in my wardrobe. I'm wearing a ravishing gown of lavender chiffon and pink roses, with the Botticelli wreath pinned in my dark curls. The received wisdom is that teagowns should only be worn on the most informal occasions but Miss Pratt tells me they are perfectly acceptable for

Eugenie's Story

dinners at home, and I shall tell my stepmother so, should she raise any objection – although I shall only come downstairs once everyone has arrived and it's too late to change. I have decided to step out of the shadows and follow my instincts rather than the stale dictates of convention. This is my time to shine.

Swallowcliffe Hall

Sunday March 19th
And now my entire world has changed. How can a single day have made so much difference? The night is quiet but I'm restless and cannot sleep. Perhaps writing down everything that has happened will allow me to examine my feelings and bring a measure of peace.

The evening did not begin well. To start with, a message had come via a footman from the Dower House to say Kate and Edward would be late, which immediately sent my father into one of his moods; he can't bear unpunctuality. I could hear him harrumphing in the hall. Shortly after that the Duxfords arrived and I came downstairs to join them in the drawing room. Mama's eyes narrowed as soon as she saw me but, as I guessed, she chose not to criticize my appearance in front of our guests. Lady Duxford must have been wearing every item of jewellery she possessed, although the evening was hardly more than a family affair, while Charlotte had chosen a nondescript dress in quite the wrong shade of blue for her complexion, with some moulting feathers stuck anyhow in her hair. One couldn't help but think of a bird's nest. Henry seemed his usual self, saying I looked 'quite splendid' as he pumped my hand clumsily in greeting.

Beyond the large picture windows the sun was setting in spectacular fashion, turning the clouds to palest pink mother-of-pearl and flooding the room

Eugenie's Story

with a golden light which sparkled on gilt picture frames, crystal chandeliers and Lady Duxford's diamonds. We were exalted, even mousy Charlotte, standing there among the treasures brought back by previous generations from their travels: Sèvres porcelain, tapestries, murky paintings by Old Masters. Did I sense even then that my life was about to take an extraordinary turn? Luckily Papa was cheering up as Henry had managed to engage him in conversation about his wall. My father's been building this extraordinary monument behind the vegetable garden for the last five years or more. Nobody can find out where it's going or what its purpose might be, but brick-laying calms him down and it's a fairly harmless eccentricity, after all. Charlotte and I were discussing the Hunt Ball — she's looking forward to it although she doesn't ride (heaven knows what she finds to do with herself all winter) — while Lady Duxford was talking to Mama about a trip to Monte Carlo from which she had just returned. So there was a hum of chatter as the Duke and his friend were announced. I didn't pay the stranger much attention at first, being only dimly aware of a dark-haired figure hovering in the background as I greeted dear Plum, whose presence is always so welcome. And then we were introduced.

His name is Patrick Hamilton-Greene. Merely writing the words gives me a shiver of excitement, as though they conjure up something of his presence.

Ridiculous, I grant, so I shall stick to the facts; those few I know. Not wanting to stare too obviously, all I can say from snatched glances is that he is the best-looking man I've ever seen. He has characteristic Irish colouring (fair skin, black hair and piercing blue eyes) and is tall and straight-backed, with a ready smile and the most delightful brogue: I found it hard to concentrate on what he was actually saying, so charming was the way he spoke. To complete the picture, he was immaculately turned out in tails with a grey silk waistcoat and a gardenia in his buttonhole.

We had only been talking for a short while before Kate and Edward appeared to join the party. As soon as I saw Kate, in a sumptuous gown of Nile-green silk trimmed around the neck with green and gold bugle beads, I wondered whether I had been wrong to choose the teagown after all, but she assured me I looked delightful. I was able to introduce her to Mr Hamilton-Greene, only too glad to let her share the conversational burden while I took a metaphorical step back to recover my composure. By means of gentle questioning, Kate discovered Mr HG was orphaned tragically young and has inherited a ramshackle castle in County Meath, not far from Dublin, overlooking the River Boyne. 'And slowly but surely sliding into it,' he says with that lovely lilt in his voice. He has come to London for a short holiday and met the Duke in the city through a mutual acquaintance. They struck up an immediate rapport. Plum mentioned he was coming down to Swallowcliffe and, thinking Mr Hamilton-Greene would like to see the house, wrote to Mama to ask whether he might be included in the party. However this tactful young man has insisted on staying at The Greyhound in Stone Martin rather than putting us to the trouble of accommodating a stranger. 'It's kind enough of your family to invite me to dinner,' he remarked, giving a slight bow. Apparently he is a keen horseman and has a cousin who runs a renowned racing stable in Ireland.

Yet what an incomplete picture is painted by these bare facts! How can I ignore the frank appreciation in the blue eyes meeting mine, the spark of electricity that passed between us as we shook hands? How can I deny the pleasure of knowing he was watching me constantly from across the dining table, even as he endeavoured to make conversation with Charlotte? I must be honest – in these pages, at least. I felt myself blossom under his gaze, hardly knowing or caring what I talked about to Henry on my right or Plum on my left. I've no idea what we ate or drank, only that course after course came and went, leaving me torn between regret the meal must eventually end, and hope that he and I would have a chance to speak again when the gentlemen came to join us after port and cigars.

As pudding arrived, however, our ship of hospitality nearly foundered on the rocks of controversy. For reasons best known to himself, Henry decided to raise the subject of Home Rule for Ireland. Edward and my father are vehemently against the Irish governing themselves. Papa unfortunately takes a jaundiced view of the race in general, having once employed a land agent from Donegal who got hold of the cellar keys and stole a case of Napoleon brandy. (Luckily he just about managed to conceal this prejudice from our guest.) Henry and Kate, it turns out, are very much in favour of Home Rule, Plum declined to comment, and Mr Hamilton-Greene can see both sides of the argument.

'Can you, by jove?' Henry exclaimed. 'In that case, you're the most extraordinarily impartial Irishman I've ever come across. Surely you feel we English have not made a tremendous success of governing you over the past few hundred years? We've taken away your land and saddled its tenant farmers with a burden of debt they can never repay. Hard to see the good in that, I'd have thought.'

'What's he saying?' demanded Papa from the other end of the table, having caught only the odd word of Henry's argument. (Thank goodness!) Edward looked furious and was, I'm sure, about to respond in kind when Charlotte of all people leapt into the breach. She told her brother that discussing politics at the dinner table was an instant route to indigestion; the men could continue their argument after we had retired, if they so chose. The look she shot him, however, suggested this would not be a good idea. Henry collected himself sufficiently to apologize but it was an extremely awkward moment. Mr Hamilton-Greene clearly only wanted to avoid offending my father and Henry would have done well to follow his example. He's not usually so thoughtless. In fact, thinking about it now, I realize Henry must be deeply jealous of this charming stranger. He's been infatuated with me since we were children. If I gave him the slightest encouragement he'd propose tomorrow but, since I've no intention of accepting, that wouldn't be fair.

In the ensuing silence, Mr Hamilton-Greene remarked gracefully, 'Now, here's an idea I'll wager we can all agree on. Who'd like to take the floor to the strains of a good old country jig? If there's a piano in the house and somebody willing to play it, I'd be happy to call the steps for a reel or two.'

There was a grateful chorus of agreement around the table and the next minute, plans had been drawn up for an impromptu dance in the library. Mr Goddard sent a couple of footmen to roll up the carpets – but who was to accompany us on the piano? Charlotte and I were agreeing to take turns when we suddenly remembered that Miss Habershon, Harriet's governess, was an accomplished musician. In due course, she was winkled out of the housekeeper's parlour (or wherever she'd been spending the evening) and proved a most willing accomplice in our merry-making. Sheet music was found for a few reels and she made a fair stab at a couple more by listening to airs hummed by Mr Hamilton-Greene. Under his instruction, we were flying around the room in great spirits, the unpleasantness of political discussion quite forgotten, and were soon so proficient that he was able to join us. Even Papa had a smile on his face before the hour was out.

How marvellous it is to dance! The joy of surrendering oneself to the music, all doubts and uncertainties cast aside, conscious of nothing but the steps one must take, the hands one will fleetingly grasp, the smiling eyes one may meet in passing. Movement, that's the thing, whether it be galloping across country on horseback or careering over a dance floor. Oh, the relief of not having to talk, or even think! And the thrill of his hand clasping mine, or resting lightly at my waist. I was a sprite, a faery flitting through enchanted lands on gauzy wings. Mrs Thompson might have had this very moment in mind when she designed my dress, and I think she would have been proud of me. Thank goodness I hadn't chosen the staid grey silk. It was worth any number of disapproving looks from Mama to be wearing my teagown this evening, of all evenings: the first time we met. I shall remember it for ever, I know.

Eventually, however, the party had to come to an end. Kate was looking pale and tired while Lady Duxford had turned practically purple in the face. Mr Hamilton-Greene kissed my hand on leaving and then Charlotte's too, for form's sake. I could hardly bear to let him go but he would not be far away, and the thought of delicious solitude to recall every glance and word that had passed between us sent me running back upstairs on winged feet. Beth was dozing on a chair outside my room, yet not even her lumpen presence could spoil my mood. At last she had finished her duties and I was free to lie alone in the dark, my heart racing and the blood pounding in my temples, certain that I would be dreaming of him as soon as I fell asleep. Every nerve in my body was tingling, alive with anticipation and delight, and his face swam before me even though my eyes were shut.

Such happy dreams they were! I can only remember brief snatches – sitting by the window at the top of a tall tower looking out over the green valley below, waltzing across a ballroom floor with his blue eyes smiling into mine, Mrs Thompson fitting me for an evening gown of cream Chantilly lace – but the overall feeling of joy has stayed with me.

*

This morning I woke early, despite the broken night's sleep, and decided to breakfast downstairs rather than in my room. After several changes of outfit, I settled for a simple frock in yellow-and-white striped cotton *piqué*, worn under a green Eton jacket with long white lapels, gilt buttons and a ripple peplum at the back. Suitably spring-like and so pretty seen from behind (an important consideration when at church). I found the Duke alone in the dining room so we breakfasted together, which was very pleasant. I was too agitated to eat a great deal but Plum helped himself liberally to kedgeree and devilled kidneys from the silver chafing dishes keeping warm over spirit lamps on the sideboard. Mama and Mrs Bragg make sure his favourite recipes are on the menu whenever he comes to stay. In fact he's more like a member of the family than a guest, having introduced my stepmother to Papa a few years after my mother died. I gather he was once an old flame of hers and he has since become a great friend of my father's too, although they are very different in character and interests. Papa would sooner hide himself away in the country whereas Plum is a leading light in London society.

My own heightened sensibility seems to have made me more aware of the happiness of others. Watching the Duke butter a slice of toast, I thought how sad it was that he and his wife should spend so much time apart. The Duchess is always abroad,

Eugenie's Story

taking a cure at some fashionable spa or other, while he loves company. One meets all sorts of fascinating people at his house in Cadogan Terrace: from diplomats and politicians to artists, actors, singers and writers. His ball to mark the end of the season is famous, and more than one marriage has been arranged in his walled garden on those balmy August nights. What a pity his own is not more companionable! He noticed me looking at him over my tea cup and smiled. 'You're very thoughtful this morning, my dear. Is anything the matter?'

I reassured him all was well with a gay laugh, whereupon he patted my hand (luckily clothed in a dainty lace glove) and said something about the exquisite torments of youth. Yes, that's it! I have become young again, reborn into a world of hope and opportunity; no conflict with Mama can be allowed to extinguish that flame. I took the opportunity to ask artlessly, 'We all found Mr Hamilton-Greene quite charming. Where did you happen to meet him?'

'I thought you would,' he replied, chuckling. 'Clara' (that's Mama) 'is always complaining about the lack of company when she's closeted away down here. I ran into him at the Garrick. He was a guest of Binkie's. Pleasant fellow, isn't he? And smartly turned-out, too. I must get the name of his tailor.'

I observed we had learned Mr Hamilton-Greene enjoyed riding and might perhaps like to take out one of our horses if he could spare the time. Plum thought that was a splendid idea but he would leave it to Mama and me to arrange the details as he had to return to London that afternoon. 'From the look of things last night, though, I'd say he'd be more than happy to extend his visit. He and your brother Edward seemed to hit it off straight away. I'm afraid Kate and Clara may end up tussling over who should entertain him.'

We laughed indulgently. That's one of the things I like most about Plum: his wryly humorous view of the world. There's usually a spark of amusement in those clever grey eyes, which don't miss a trick yet seem to accept his friends' little foibles with tolerant kindness.

After breakfast, the minutes passed agonizingly slowly until it was time for church. I paced up and down in my bedroom, trying on hats. Mr Hamilton-Greene would surely be there. What could we talk about? How would I respond to his overtures? One must maintain a ladylike composure, of course, but surely there had to be some acknowledgement of what had passed between us the night before. What if he chose not to attend the service? He might be a Catholic or belong to a strange Irish sect. But no, Plum would never have brought him to Swallowcliffe if that were the case. I had nobody to ask for guidance, not being able to confide in Mama and with Kate so wrapped up in her own affairs these days. Somehow we've never become as close as I once hoped we would, although Kate is closer to me in age than Harriet and we have so much more in common.

At long last our party set off in the barouche – apart from Mama, who was indisposed. Miss Habershon was telling Harriet about our party of the night before; I hope she doesn't assume she'll be included in all such social occasions. In fact I shouldn't think she will be with us much longer, since John is away at boarding school and Harriet must surely have learnt everything there is to know by now. Still, at least she is a quiet and unobtrusive young woman.

Then finally the moment had arrived, and we were walking into church, and there he was, sitting between Edward and Kate in the second family pew. One glance was all it took to set my heart pounding anew and tell me the night before had been no illusion. If anything, he was even more handsome than I remembered. I managed to smile calmly enough as we took our places and knelt in quiet devotion but, feeling his gaze on the back of my neck, I found it hard to concentrate on the sermon or prayers and faltered at the start of the first hymn. Yet I soon recovered, sending my voice flying up to the vaulted ceiling of our little church: one of the oldest in England, with a square Norman tower, foundations dating back to Saxon times and the most glorious stained-glass windows. I heard him join in behind me, and the rest of the congregation faded away until the two of us might have been singing alone together. It was quite magical.

At the end of the service we filed out into the fresh air and stood about, chatting inconsequentially. Mr Hamilton-Greene thanked my father for such a wonderful evening, and hoped my stepmother would soon be feeling better, and that I had enjoyed the dancing. I could think of nothing particular to say, beyond commenting on the weather which has been absolutely glorious so far this spring. And then Edward clapped him on the back and announced that 'HG', as he called him, was to stay for a few days with them at the Dower House. They had a certain business proposal to discuss and HG would be the perfect riding companion for Kate (my brother not liking horses). She didn't seem particularly enthusiastic about the idea, however. Although she smiled when Edward had finished speaking, she looked strained and ill-at-ease.

I cast about for a means of conveying to Mr Hamilton-Greene my happiness at this news and my own love of exploring the countryside on horseback. It was difficult in company, but suddenly our chance presented itself. Kate walked off a little way to talk to some worthy indigent and I found myself following at a suitable distance. Catching up with me, Mr Hamilton-Greene took off his hat and asked in a low, urgent voice, 'Perhaps we may meet again, Miss Vye, in the near future?' The colour rose in my cheeks; there was no point in pretending not to understand. I stammered something about being at home for calls most afternoons this week but of course then he would have to converse with Mama also. And he has already seen my teagown.

It was Kate who unwittingly came to our rescue. 'I have arranged to call on Mrs Beamish tomorrow afternoon,' she said, rejoining us. 'If you don't mind interrupting our tour of the village with a quick detour, Mr Hamilton-Greene? We needn't stay long.'

I saw my chance and seized it with both hands. 'Why, Mrs Bragg has made some calf's foot jelly for the Beamishes,' I said smoothly. 'I was planning to take it over some time next week. Perhaps we could visit Mrs Beamish together, to avoid disturbing her more than necessary?'

And so it was arranged. Tomorrow I shall see him again, and perhaps while Kate is busy with the Beamishes, we may find another occasion to speak privately. There is so much I need to find out: how long he's planning to stay at the Dower House, whether he'll still be in London when we are there for the season, the nature of the business he and Edward have embarked upon together. All I know for certain is that I have an admirer, one who has awakened feelings in me I feared had vanished for ever. And India suddenly seems very far away.

Monday March 20th

An unsatisfactory day on several accounts. This morning Beth was unable to persuade Mrs Bragg to part with any calf's foot jelly, although I'm sure there's a plentiful supply in the still room. After I'd sent Beth back to the kitchen a second time, she returned with a small jar of grapefruit marmalade – far less appropriate. I can't imagine the Beamishes are great marmalade eaters, grapefruit or otherwise. However I was too preoccupied by the prospect of seeing him again to worry about that. I'd chosen to wear the navy-blue skirt Beth has just finished remodelling, with a striped lawn blouse and grey cape trimmed with navy braid. (The sleeves of dresses are so large now, it's impossible to fit a jacket comfortably over them.) This sober outfit was transformed by a delightful new hat from Hooper and Ruscoe's in Regent Street: navy straw trimmed with rosettes of pink satin ribbon, a band of pink ribbon round the crown and a Josephine plume at the side.

On the way to the Dower House I happened to spot my father at work on his wall and seized the moment to talk to him. 'The thing is, Papa,' I began, once we had exchanged the usual pleasantries, 'you may think clothes are inconsequential but they are more important to me now than ever before. The right frock is crucial. To appear in an outdated gown is tantamount to throwing in the towel, retiring from the race, hoisting a white flag. I simply can't hold up my head in last year's fashions.'

He sat back on his heels, puffing on his pipe between clenched teeth as he stared at the interminable brickwork. I had no idea whether he understood or, frankly, had even been listening. 'Would you consider raising my allowance to a hundred guineas?' I asked finally in desperation. 'Or even seventy-five? Think of it as an investment in my future.'

'Now look here, Button,' he began, removing the pipe for a moment, 'in an ideal world everyone would have exactly what he or she wanted – all of us, from myself and your mama down to Harry the hall boy. I would have an endless supply of Staffordshire Blues for the patterns on my wall, instead of having to scratch about the brickworks for remnants, and Harry would have as much mild ale as he could drink without falling over. But we don't live in an ideal world. We inhabit this imperfect one, where compromises have to be made. I'm sorry, old girl, but no can do as far as extra funds are concerned.' He replaced the pipe and sucked busily away before picking up his trowel. 'You always look jolly smart, anyway. Pass me the cement bucket, would you?'

It's all very well for Papa to talk about compromise, I thought bitterly, resuming the path; he does exactly as he pleases. This wretched wall of his must have cost hundreds of pounds so far and it serves no purpose whatsoever, beyond enraging

Woodford who liked to use that patch of ground for bonfires. And as for Mama! She's never been known to deny herself anything.

Vigorous exercise and anticipation of the significant meeting ahead calmed my temper, however, and my anger had subsided a little by the time I arrived at the Dower House and was shown into the drawing-room. It's looking very fresh and pretty these days, I must say. The walls have been hung with pale-blue damask and the ceiling painted cream with the cornice, decorations and central rose picked out in gold: like a piece of gilded Wedgewood china. Kate has replaced the dark oak furniture with French pieces in a lighter style which suit the room very well, although a cream sofa and armchairs are hardly practical.

I had plenty of time to examine the furnishings before Kate appeared – alone. She informed me casually that Mr Hamilton-Greene would not be joining us, as the gentlemen had gone to London this morning for a meeting at the bank. Just like that, with no thought of my disappointment on hearing the news! And she had packed such an embarrassingly large basket of provisions for the Beamishes that we had to take the gig instead of walking, which I had very much wanted to do as it was another lovely day. So all in all, I was hardly in the best frame of mind for a charitable visit.

The Beamishes live in the middle one of three

farmworkers' cottages on the outskirts of Stone Martin. The front step had been freshly scrubbed and whitened but inside, the house smelt so musty and stale, I longed to throw open the windows and give it a thorough airing. We were shown into the front parlour by Mrs Beamish, an anxious woman with bad teeth and red-knuckled hands in a shabby print frock. Far too old to be still having babies, surely. She was overwhelmed by the hamper and kept dropping curtseys as its contents were unloaded: shoes for the children, liniment, vegetables, blankets – and of course the grapefruit marmalade, for which she thanked me so profusely, I began to wish I'd never brought it. There was no sign of the incapacitated Mr Beamish, who she said was 'still rather poorly', but the many Beamish children were duly summoned and presented for our approval: pale, long-legged creatures the spit of their mother in various sizes. They were quickly dismissed, not to be seen again during our visit, although at one point I noticed a tousled head watching us through the front window which immediately ducked out of sight. Kate asked after the baby, whose chest had apparently been a worry; for want of anything better to do, I suggested we might have a look at it.

Mrs Beamish seemed oddly reluctant to show us into the kitchen, where the baby was sleeping, and the reason for this soon became clear. It was perfectly horrid: dark and low-ceilinged, furnished only by a dusty range along one wall, a table covered with newspaper pushed against the other, a chair in the corner containing a grimy old person (introduced *sotto voce* as Mr Beamish's mother), and a box on the floor containing the baby. Laundry hung on a line across the room, although it would surely have dried more quickly outside, and there was an odd smell in the air, both sickly-sweet and rotten. A couple of flies were buzzing at the window pane as if desperate to escape. I could sympathize. The floor was sticky and something crunched under my foot that might once have been alive.

We dutifully inspected the baby. 'Please don't disturb her,' Kate said to Mrs Beamish, who'd made as if to pick it up. 'She looks so peaceful.'

'The goose fat worked wonders, M'Lady,' Mrs Beamish said, curtseying again. 'Thank you so much, Ma'am. I don't know what we should have done without you, honestly I don't.' There was something repellent about her manner, like that of a beaten dog fawning before its master. Casting my eyes round the room, I caught sight of the one lovely thing in it – a bright red geranium in a pot on the windowsill – and tried to hold it in my mind as a talisman against the squalor for the rest of our visit.

'I do feel sorry for the poor woman,' Kate said, when at last we were driving back to civilization. 'I'm glad you met her, Eugenie. Now you can see why I want to do something for the tenants.'

Yet surely they should want to do something for themselves! Mrs Beamish might be poor but it doesn't cost anything to roll up one's sleeves and wash the floor. I'd be ashamed to let a house of mine get into such a state. Kate was having none of it, however. 'Who knows what we'd do in her position?' she said 'The poor woman's exhausted. It's as much as she can do to keep the children washed and fed.' Nobody asked her to have so many of them, though. I couldn't help thinking Mrs Beamish herself was mainly responsible for her own trials and tribulations.

We were passing the derelict barn at this point. Kate pulled up the horse and we stared at it for a moment in silence. Of course, I thought, that's it: Edward's poured cold water on the almshouse plan and she wants to enlist my help in pleading her cause. I was about to make it clear I wouldn't dream of stepping between man and wife when I saw to my dismay that Kate was crying. Now came my turn to play the comforter, which I tried my best to do, telling her she must think of herself and take a rest from these depressing charitable schemes and visits. 'There's no point upsetting yourself on the Beamishes' account,' I said. 'Whatever you do for people like that, they'll always have too many children, waste what little money they have and make life difficult for themselves.'

'No,' she replied obstinately, dashing away her

tears. 'I'm not giving up. All Mrs Beamish needs is some hope, a helping hand towards the light at the end of the tunnel. Surely that's not too much to ask? It's just that I feel very far away from home sometimes, especially when things are difficult, and I miss my mother.'

'At least you have a mother to miss,' I pointed out gently, 'unlike some of us. And there are lots of lovely things on the horizon to look forward to. It'll be Easter soon and the Hunt Ball, and then before you know it your aunt and cousin will be here, and you'll be guiding them through the hustle and bustle of a London season, with balls, and gay little supper parties, and riding through Hyde Park in that elegant Busvine habit that shows off your figure to perfection. Not to mention the gorgeous gowns Mrs Thompson is making for us!'

Eventually she smiled and said I was a perfect tonic, and we drove off much more happily. I've always had the knack of cheering people up. Kate has her head in the clouds, that's all, and she's been spending too much time in dark, dreary places. She'll come to accept the way of the world sooner or later.

*

It was a relief to sit in the drawing room at the Dower House with a well-earned cup of tea. But, ugh! I had to wash my hands several times first in one of the many bathrooms. It felt as though tiny

Eugenie's Story

creatures were crawling over my skin and even through the roots of my hair. Drying my hands afterwards, I found myself thinking about that bright scarlet flower flaring against the dirty windowpane, wondering what impulse had led Mrs Beamish to put it there and what she thought when she looked at it. It's not that I'm insensible to the sufferings of others – quite the opposite. If anything, I feel too deeply, and must struggle to contain emotions that would otherwise be overwhelming. Kate's right: Mrs Beamish is so entirely different from us, we can't possibly put ourselves in her shoes. And I suppose if you've never developed a taste for beautiful things, you don't miss them.

Still no sign of the gentlemen returning. Why had Edward rushed Mr HG away so suddenly, without even the chance to leave me a note? Waiting like this with so many unanswered questions was unbearably tantalizing, and still no hint of an invitation to dinner or any other sort of occasion at the Dower House. 'What a delightful evening we spent together the other night,' I offered eventually. 'Perhaps we might suggest to the committee that some jigs are played at the Hunt Ball, if a caller could be found? I suppose Mr Hamilton-Greene will have left us by then.'

Kate replied she didn't know what his plans were. 'I have my reservations about that particular young man,' she said. 'He seems a little insubstantial to me.'

'How can you say such a thing?' I exclaimed. 'He's a man of property, even if he has no title, and Edward's business partner! If Edward trusts him, so should we.'

'There's a long way to go before he and Edward become business partners,' she replied tartly. 'And you have to admit, Mr Hamilton-Greene is something of an unknown quantity. He seems rather a fly-by-night when compared to someone like Henry Duxford, for example.'

So she's been recruited to the Duxford cause! 'Henry Duxford is a treasured friend, of course,' I replied stiffly, 'but one could compare him to a book one has read several times. A new acquaintance is a volume with its pages uncut, full of undiscovered treasures.'

An apt metaphor, I thought, but Kate merely sighed and patted my hand in a way I found rather patronizing. She of all people ought to understand my feelings, having married into a foreign culture herself. After all, surely what matters most is that leap of the heart, that passionate thrill at the sight of a particular face or the sound of a certain voice, which comes but rarely in a lifetime – as I know to my cost.

'All right then,' she said suddenly, as though granting a concession. 'Mr Hamilton-Greene and I have arranged to go riding tomorrow morning before breakfast. Why don't you join us?'

I accepted, although it was a very last-minute invitation. It is only now, as I write this account in the quiet of my room, that a disturbing thought occurs to me. Does Kate have designs on Mr Hamilton-Greene herself? Is she hoping to throw me off the scent with these trumped-up suspicions? It seems odd the two of them should be going out together alone, given her remarks about him. Perhaps she's jealous of his feelings for me, and trying to come between us...

Well, no doubt I shall find out tomorrow.

Tuesday March 21ˢᵗ

I'm almost ashamed to re-read my previous remarks, knowing what I know now, and yet it was only ignorance that caused me to make them. I shouldn't judge myself too harshly. Tempting as it is to rewrite history with the benefit of hindsight, the record must stand so I can look back at my true feelings in, say, a year's time. Where shall I be then? No longer at Swallowcliffe, that's the only thing for certain.

I was up early this morning, dressed in my riding habit, soft leather gloves and top hat tied with a jaunty band of black net that streams out behind at the gallop. I love an early-morning ride when the world is just waking up and the fields are quiet and still, shrouded ankle-deep in a blanket of mist. Zoffany shook his head and whinnied, as if to say it had been too long since we'd been off adventuring together. A rabbit scuttered away into the long grass with a flash of its white tail, alarmed by the clatter of hooves, but a steady hand on the reins brought my horse quickly back under control. I was filled with a calm quiet certainty, trotting down the drive in happy anticipation.

They were riding out of the stables as I approached, Kate's hunter Tybalt shying at a wheelbarrow left in the yard. Kate seemed a little preoccupied but, I must confess, I wasn't paying her a great deal of attention at that point. All I could see was how elegantly he rode, and how splendid he looked on horseback: mounted on the grey mare my brother Rory keeps stabled at the Dower House. Innate breeding will always shine through. He said how sorry he was not to have seen me yesterday, although there was no need for the apology. Of course business must be the first priority and I know how insistent (sometimes even unreasonable) Edward can be.

We set off through the park towards a broad avenue of oak trees that leads up to the Fairview Tower, from where one can ride for miles along the hilltop through woodland paths and open fields, until on a clear day one may catch a distant glimpse of the sea. 'Did you ever see such a view?' he exclaimed, standing up in the stirrups to look around, and I felt prouder of the familiar landscape than ever, seeing it afresh through his eyes. My blood was up, the sun was on my cheeks and he was close beside me as we galloped through the glorious morning, Kate a little way behind. There was no room for anything in my mind but his presence, his warm smile, his broad shoulders and strong hands holding the reins, so commanding yet so responsive too.

Eventually we reined in the horses at a gate, quite out of breath, and looked behind to see – nothing but empty fields. Where was Kate? At first I assumed she was being tactfully discreet, allowing us a little time alone to get to know each other, but Mr Hamilton-Greene felt we should ride back in case she'd had an accident or some other mishap had occurred. Just as well, as things turned out. As we retraced our steps and realized how far she had fallen behind, I began to grow anxious too, imagining all sorts of possible disasters. We eventually found her a mile or two back, leaning against a hedge while Tybalt cropped the grass beside her. Apparently she'd been feeling increasingly unwell but hadn't called out to us, being reluctant to make a fuss (although it would have saved a great deal of trouble if she had). Unfortunately she didn't feel able to continue riding, even though I offered to swap horses as Zoffany is much steadier than Tybalt. Mr Hamilton-Greene said he would fetch help from a farm in the valley below if I could look after Kate until he returned, and that seemed the only possible course of action. She was shivering so he gallantly wrapped his hacking jacket around her shoulders.

After he'd left, Kate still seemed reluctant to explain exactly what was wrong but asked me to help her across the field so she could sit on the stile. As feminine intuition came into play, I began to realize this indisposition was no mere dizzy spell but something more serious; she had turned very pale and was clearly in some pain. She seemed to be suffering from such indisposition as women are sometimes called upon to bear, by nature of our sex. I merely soothed her as much as I could, telling her help was on its way and she would soon be right as rain. There's a certain sweetness to be found in giving comfort, so gratefully received; it's not a role one is often required or allowed to play. I felt very close to her, almost motherly, as she laid her head against my shoulder, clutching my hand so tightly that my fingers grew numb. I don't normally like having my hands touched but on this occasion it would have been churlish to object.

At last, after what seemed an interminable wait, we saw a farm cart bumping its way towards us with our knight in shining armour riding alongside it. He thought Kate and I should be taken down to the farm while he raced back to the Dower House to tell Edward what had happened and arrange for a carriage to bring her home. So a farmhand took our horses down the hill, we were helped into the cart, and off it set down the rutted track. Poor Kate couldn't help wincing at every bump and jolt of that tortuous journey, but I wrapped my arms around her and tried to hold her steady as best I could. We must have made a pretty picture.

Luckily the farm was a clean, well-kept sort of place, obviously owned by decent people. The farmer's wife came running out to meet us and helped Kate into the kitchen, making her as comfortable as possible on an oak settle piled with cushions, and giving her a nip of brandy. She lay back, eyes closed, while I wiped her brow with a handkerchief dipped in eau-de-cologne. That's what I should have liked, were I in her position. It was clear she needed medical attention and thank goodness, when Edward appeared with the landau, he said that Mr Hamilton-Greene had already ridden to summon the doctor.

Whatever should we have done without him? He rose to the occasion unhesitatingly, with all the command, tact and discretion of a true gentleman. There can be no further doubt about his character: he has been tested and not found wanting. My brother also showed as much sympathy as anyone could possibly have wished. Sometimes he seems a little remote but on this occasion he played the part of concerned husband to perfection, rushing to Kate's side and scooping her up in his arms. No one could blame her for the tears that were only then allowed to flow as she was carried out to the carriage and lifted inside. I had thought she might want to keep me at her side but it wasn't my place to insist, and I didn't need to be thanked for my small part in the proceedings. One of the grooms had been brought along to ride Tybalt home and provide an escort for me. Exhausted though I was, my duty was clearly to take Zoffany back to Swallowcliffe, explain what had happened and wait for further news from the Dower House. We were on the point of leaving when the farmer's wife rushed out with Mr Hamilton-Greene's jacket, forgotten in the rush. I was cold now so I took the opportunity to borrow it myself (Harris tweed, I saw from the label), finding the rough warmth of the wool reassuring. Thrusting my chilled hand into one of the pockets – my gloves having somehow been mislaid in the crisis – my fingers came across a folded piece of paper which I surreptitiously tucked into my sleeve for later examination. However on scanning the note quickly later, it turned out to be no more romantic or enlightening than a bill for horse feed: oats, bran, that sort of thing, and liniment for strained muscles.

Breakfast was long over by the time I returned to the Hall. I found Mama in the housekeeper's parlour, discussing arrangements with Mrs Henderson for Easter. What a cool character she is! There was precious little sympathy for either Kate or myself after the ordeal we had suffered, merely a sense of disappointment and the drily-expressed observation that Swallowcliffe would evidently have to wait a while longer for an heir to inherit from Edward. An astonishing and, I felt, somewhat coarse remark. How could anyone show such a lack of fellow-feeling? Any hope I might once have had that we could one day lay aside our differences and come to an understanding was finally extinguished. Whatever the crisis, Mama can think only of her own interests.

I, on the other hand, was limp, exhausted by emotion and longing to confide in someone. With Kate *hors de combat*, I felt very much alone. Harriet's too young and peculiar, while Charlotte would only have delivered some dreary homily about the dangers of horse-riding. The Galbraiths and their set live too far away to see very often, and since Connie left and Mary married her curate, my social circle has become sadly diminished. It's been months since I last heard from Araminta. She and I were like sisters once, as we would have become once Freddie and I were married, but his passing created a rift between us. When I looked to her for sympathy she seemed almost affronted, as though she were the only one allowed to mourn. Yet surely a fiancée has as much right to grieve as a sister. I was disappointed by her reaction and she must have sensed that and drawn further away, to a dark place where I could not reach her. Maybe she even blamed me for what happened? No, I cannot allow myself to think so; that way madness lies. It was a cruel act of fate that sent my beloved into the path of a runaway gig on his way to see me, and no one can be held responsible. Except Freddie himself, I suppose, but it seems harsh to judge him when he was to pay so dearly for one moment of absent-mindedness when crossing the road.

I was thankful that for once Beth attended me promptly this afternoon, suggesting a cooling soak in Epsom Salts for my hands, which had suffered from such a long ride, followed by a rest until it was time for tea. She also showed me an advertisement for the most ingenious invention. *'La Merveilleuse'*,

Eugenie's Story

it's called: a light wire frame covered with hair in a choice of shades to match one's own. Very modern and hygienic. Ever since our visit to the Beamishes, my scalp has become unnaturally itchy and I can't shake off the notion that I may have acquired some sort of infestation, although Beth has washed and disinfected the false hair pads several times and combed through my own with no trace of unwanted visitors. She tells me in her earthy way that horse sweat is a proven remedy in these cases but I don't think such desperate measures are required just yet.

After a nap I felt somewhat restored and my spirits were lifted still further by changing into the lovely teagown. Of course! I suddenly realized that Mrs Thompson is the ideal person to act as my confidante and adviser; she's so discreetly sympathetic, and I need to visit her soon for a fitting anyway. I may even ask her to treat Kate's order as a priority rather than mine. New frocks are always so cheering, and it would be a small sacrifice to make.

When shall I see him again? I can't decide whether to wait here for news tomorrow or call at the Dower House myself. The only thing to be said of this dreadful experience is that it has bound us closer; we have faced the storm and weathered it together.

Swallowcliffe Hall

Thursday March 23rd
What sort of person have I become? A determined, cold-eyed young woman looks back at me from the mirror: beautiful, yes, but hard-hearted. It is Mama who has changed me, forced me to match her cunning stroke for stroke in this strange and subtle game we are playing. Yet sweet girlish Eugenie has not gone for good; she is merely biding her time. When I am mistress of my own destiny she will emerge again, like a butterfly casting off the chrysalis.

    Mr Hamilton-Greene has come to see me, and we have moved closer to declaring our true feelings for each other. Yesterday morning I was distracting myself by playing the piano in the drawing room, wearing a gown of China silk in the 1830s style with a dear little zouave jacket. Somehow I must have sensed he would come to us because it was an inappropriate outfit for walking, although of course I could have taken a carriage to the Dower House or changed into something more suitable for a call on foot. At any rate, I happened to catch sight of him striding up to the front door and, desperate for news, rushed out to meet him in the hall: an unladylike eagerness that was surely understandable in the circumstances. In a few words he told me that Kate was no longer in any danger but in need of peace and quiet, and he had decided to return to lodgings in the village rather than presume on his friends' hospitality a moment longer. 'So I'll not be far away, Miss Vye,' he said, with a significant look from those remarkable blue eyes. 'Perhaps I could drop by another day? The afternoon might be a better time, I'm thinking.'

I agreed at once to this modest request. We were somewhat constrained by the presence of the servants: a footman stationed by the front door, Mr Goddard, fussing about with calling cards on the hall table, Perkins taking advantage of my absence to riddle the drawing-room fire with much clattering and clanking of the poker. There was so much more that needed to be said but neither of us could bring ourselves to begin. 'I do hope you'll find The Greyhound comfortable,' I blurted out at last. He said he hoped so too and replaced his hat. At once the footman sprang to open the door, and only then did I notice the envelope in his hand, which instead of laying on the salver Goddard was holding, he gave directly to me. 'I've taken the liberty of writing to you, Miss Vye,' he said in a low voice. 'Maybe when you've a moment...'

I hardly knew what to reply but managed to stammer assent. With a nod he strode towards the door, shoulders squared and head held high: every inch the gentleman. I watched him go in a sort of stupor before fleeing upstairs to the sanctuary of my room, the precious envelope clutched tight against my pounding heart.

Unfortunately Mama was lying in wait for me

on the landing. 'What on earth – ?' she began, but I would not stop and hurried on down the corridor, her footsteps hot on my heels. To my horror, she followed me into my bedroom before I could close the door. Beth, who happened to be tidying frocks in my wardrobe, looked round at us in alarm.

'Have you taken leave of your senses?' Mama hissed when I turned to confront her, hiding the letter behind my back. 'What do you mean by receiving callers alone? And at this hour of the day?'

'Not just any caller,' I retorted. 'Mr Hamilton-Greene brought news of Kate, in case you'd forgotten about her. She is out of danger, you'll be glad to hear.'

'Enough! I will not be spoken to in this way.' Mama was quivering with fury but a strange calm had descended on me; the more emotion she displayed, the easier I found it to control my own feelings. No doubt sensing my advantage, she took a couple of breaths to steady herself. 'Give me the letter,' she demanded, reaching out for it.

Whereupon the most extraordinary thing happened: I felt the envelope taken from me by unseen fingers. 'What letter?' I was able to counter.

'The one you're attempting to conceal,' she replied. This time I was more than willing to show her my hands: the palms flaking a little, but incontrovertibly empty. She stared at me suspiciously and then around the room, only now seeming to notice Beth, who looked back at us with her habitual blank stare. I was seized with a wild impulse to laugh but thankfully managed to restrain myself.

'Why would you think I have a letter?' I said boldly. 'Surely you haven't been listening to a private conversation, Mama?'

In retrospect that might have been a step too far. 'You are not entitled to private conversations,' she snapped. 'This is my house and you'll obey my rules while you live in it. I don't know what's the matter with you, young lady! The one time in your life when you can least afford to put a foot wrong, you seem determined to act the giddy goat.'

Sensing the danger I was in, I lowered my eyes and murmured an apology.

'I'm worried for you, truly I am,' Mama continued. 'Sometimes you seem almost unhinged. All this twitching and fidgeting and rushing about, these silly outbursts and secret schemes... Not to mention the way you deliberately flout my instructions. It might be best if you went away somewhere for a long rest: perhaps an English resort in some secluded place which offers treatment for the nerves. Hydrotherapy is said to be most efficacious. You can't possibly go to India in this state – who knows what might happen in such a climate.'

Her words sent a chill down my spine. 'Please don't concern yourself on my behalf,' I begged. 'I'm perfectly well, only a little unsettled by what happened yesterday.'

She looked at me for a long while as if making up her mind. I returned her gaze, reminding myself it was only jealousy that made her speak so harshly. Her hair is still dark but a streak of pure white has recently appeared at the front; some people consider it striking but it merely makes me think of a badger. 'As it happens, I've received a note from Lord McGillie,' she said at last. 'He tells me he will be spending Easter with his aunt and is hoping to see us all at the Hunt Ball, which they will be attending. A charming and respectable letter, as one might expect, quite properly addressed to me. Lord McGillie has breeding and knows how to behave.'

Once upon a time this news might have thrilled me, but the only letter I could think of now was the one hidden, I hoped, in Beth's apron pocket. Lord McGillie might know how to behave but it is Mr Hamilton-Greene who has captured my heart.

'Until then,' Mama went on, 'you are to conduct yourself with the utmost decorum. You will go nowhere and see no one without my permission, and you will act with discretion at all times; or at least try to. Is that understood?'

'Yes, Mama,' I said demurely, my head lowered.

'Charlotte Duxford would be a good influence. I suggest you spend some time with her: sketching, perhaps, or playing music. I shall be watching you carefully over the next couple of weeks. You will come to my room every morning and tell me your plans for the day.'

Such lack of trust! But what am I to do? Until I marry, my life is not my own.

When Mama had gone, Beth and I were left face to face. Wordlessly she held out the letter to me, still with the same inscrutable expression. I took it, wondering how to acknowledge her help. After all, she had put herself out for me at some personal risk. 'Thank you, Beth,' I said eventually. 'That was very quick-witted of you.'

'It's all right, Miss,' she replied. 'Why shouldn't you keep a few secrets to yourself?'

The familiar tone of her voice grated somewhat, and I was itching for her to leave so I could read my letter in private. 'Well, now I'd like to rest,' I told her briskly, 'but perhaps you could attend to me in half an hour or so. It might be soothing if you were to brush my hair. You're not nearly as heavy-handed as you used to be.' I was gratified to see her blush with pleasure at the compliment as she backed carefully out of the room, trying not to knock anything over as unfortunately so often happens.

Alone at last, I tore open the envelope with trembling fingers and unfolded the familiar sheet of cream paper inside, embossed with the Vye family crest. I could picture him sitting down to write in the Willow Room at the Dower House, pouring out his heart on the page. This is what he said:

Swallowcliffe Hall

My dear Miss Vye

You must be worried about Mrs Vye but your brother tells me she is quite comfortable, just in need of some rest. In the circumstances I thought it best to give them some privacy and will take a room at The Greyhound in Stone Martin until our business is finished. I'm fixed on going to the Hunt Ball which sounds a good old shindig and hope to see you then if not before. Perhaps I might call on you one afternoon, if time permits?

Sure but I'm glad you were there yesterday! You were a ministering angel and no mistake.

Your obedient servant,
Patrick Hamilton-Greene

His handwriting is a little difficult to read, admittedly, but I was charmed by the sentiments expressed. One might have thought a letter unnecessary since he had told me most of this information in person, but I could read between the lines. He particularly wanted me to know he would be attending the Hunt Ball, and that he would not be far away until then.

'A ministering angel'! It's as though he can see into my very soul.

Eugenie's Story

Friday March 31ˢᵗ
Thus far I'm succeeding admirably in my strategy of lying low and busying myself with worthy tasks so Mama's suspicions are allayed. Here's how I've been spending the past week:

Saturday: I visit Kate, having sent an enquiry the day before to find out whether she is receiving calls. I bring Calla lilies from the hothouse, milk of cucumber soap, some magazines and a novel, and wear my ivory silk gown and a large Leghorn hat trimmed with pink roses. Kate is reclining in bed, sporting a delectable lace *peignoir*; her room is chock full of flowers. She's looking better than I've seen her for months: not just well, but happier and calmer in spirits. She tells me Edward has been most attentive. From the look of her this must be true and I'm thankful to hear it, for all our sakes. Without prompting, she goes on to say they are both most grateful to Mr Hamilton-Greene and I for rescuing her, and that Edward and HG (as they call him) are forging ahead with their business plans. What wonderful news! However she thinks it best for HG to stay in the village for the time being as Edward does not want her overtired. I do not say anything about his letter to me and act surprised, secretly rejoicing she can now see him in his true colours.

I read to her for a while from the novel I've brought but become excessively sleepy, so we agree to switch to *The Lady* magazine instead. Minuet balls are all the rage in London, we learn; the dancers require a lot of space so benches rather than chairs are provided for chaperones. I wonder what Aunt Georgina, who suffers from sciatica, will think of that. After some pleasant speculation about the season ahead and the imminent arrival of Kate's aunt and cousin (who've set sail from New York and are due to arrive in about ten days' time), I take my leave. As I kiss my dear sister goodbye, inspiration strikes and I offer to visit Mrs Beamish while she's laid low. Her face lights up and we part on the closest of terms. His words echo in my head: I am truly 'a ministering angel', and beginning to enjoy the role.

Sunday: Church, but he is not there. I wear a fawn silk gown and my zouave jacket – all for nothing. Mama is grim-faced at luncheon; she and my father barely speak. I imagine she may have broached the subject of sending me away to a clinic and he has refused to countenance it, and try to express my appreciation indirectly through smiles and nods. He does not respond. Another sunny day and in the afternoon I stroll about the park with Harriet while she tries to catch butterflies. What an odd girl she is.

Monday: I visit the Beamishes, with qualified success. Bearing the mourning gowns Miss Pratt has deemed beyond salvation, I knock on their front door for some minutes before Mrs Beamish eventually emerges, sleeves rolled up and hair falling down at the back. Apparently it's wash day. Inside, the cottage is in chaos: there are children tumbling about all over the place and the baby is wailing. Mrs B takes me into the front room, where the furniture is now covered in dustsheets, but has to keep darting back to the kitchen as the copper's boiling over. I'm not offered any refreshment, and when I unpack the parcel to show her the mourning gowns, she starts to cry. It soon becomes clear these are not tears of gratitude, as I initially assumed. One of the children sidles into the room to stare at me but runs away when I attempt to engage it in conversation. Feeling a little *de trop*, I take my leave as soon as decently possible, promising to return another day; Mrs Beamish is clearly relieved. Despite the best of intentions, I fear I lack the common touch.

Tuesday: Receive a note from Mrs Thompson advising my ballgown is ready and inviting me for a final fitting in their new *atelier* on Saturday. Mama reluctant to accompany me but finally agrees I may go alone with Beth, straight there and back. Call on Charlotte in the afternoon, wearing a cream and black pin-striped shirtwaist refashioned with new sleeves and bodice, and a black straw hat lined in cream satin edged with jet. Duxford House as grim as ever. Charlotte has to ring repeatedly for more jam to accompany the scones. Lady D is out at a committee meeting but Henry takes a cup of tea with us and asks whether I'm attending the Hunt Ball (of course he knows I am). Agree to save him at least one dance and think how lovely it is to have admirers, even those whose hopes I must ultimately disappoint. I accompany Charlotte on the piano (she likes to sing) and we decide to go sketching on Thursday.

Wednesday: A dull day. I go for a drive in the morning with Harriet and Mama; we pass The Greyhound but there's no sign of Mr HG. I haven't seen him for days. Why hasn't he visited? In the afternoon John arrives home for the Easter holidays, so much more grown-up in long trousers and a serious expression – which soon gives way to one of joy as he rushes from one favourite place to another. He spends a long time in the stables, telling Dobbin about boarding school. Kate calls in the afternoon, still a little pale but clearly on the mend. She says sadly Mr Beamish passed away yesterday, owing to complications from his injury. How prescient of me to have taken round the mourning gowns! Mrs Beamish is relieved of one worry at least. I'm tormented again by a horridly itchy scalp and feel this can hardly be a coincidence. Attempt to distract myself with scrapbooking and embroidery.

Thursday: Charlotte and Henry both arrive for

sketching! Mama is clearly put out but she can hardly send Henry away and after all, I had no idea he was coming. I suggest we attempt a view of the village with the river in the foreground, and we set off for a suitable spot near the western edge of the park. The sun is beating down again so Charlotte and I take parasols. This spring is truly more like summer. Henry clad in a straw hat and artist's smock which strikes me as pretentious but it turns out he's quite an accomplished watercolourist. Painting has never seemed a particularly manly occupation to me. I can't settle and am further distracted by the sight of a gentleman emerging from The Greyhound and walking off towards the Dower House. I'm pretty sure it's Mr Hamilton-Greene but the figure is too small to be certain. It is torture to know he's so near and yet out of reach. Also the desire to scratch my head becomes overwhelming; I have to get up and walk about in an effort to calm myself. Henry asks me if anything is the matter. Thank goodness eventually a footman arrives with a basket of provisions and we abandon our easels for a surprisingly jolly picnic. I tell Charlotte my brother Rory is soon arriving for Easter and she blushes. The conversation turns to the subject of Mrs Thompson and Botticelli wreaths, and I invite her to accompany me to London for the fitting on Saturday. Mrs Thompson will be grateful for the introduction, Charlotte will have her eyes opened and Mama will be reassured I have a companion: an excellent plan all round. Henry is clearly bored and starts talking about a series of political essays he's writing. I find it hard to feign interest. Still, at least when he's talking about serious matters we don't have to hear that dreadful guffaw.

*

And now today is Good Friday, a time for solemn reflection. We are spending a quiet Easter: for the first time in years we have no house guests, not even the Duke. (Rory is family and doesn't count.) Mama is still hostile but I tell myself I'll soon be free of her for good. Tomorrow I shall see my ballgown and consult with that guardian angel, Mrs Thompson. In the meantime the only thing is to watch and wait, preparing myself for next Friday while remaining vigilant should Mr Hamilton-Greene find a chance to call. Yet it's hard to be patient when my whole future is at stake.

Saturday April 1ˢᵗ
Extremely agitated. Have received news which will take some time to digest. Hands bad.

Sunday April 2ⁿᵈ
So. Having had time to reflect, I am now able to relate what has occurred. 'Emotions recollected in tranquility,' as Wordsworth aptly puts it, although the blessed state of tranquility still escapes me.

Yesterday Thomas took Beth and me to the station for our journey to London, where we met Charlotte and Henry, who had gallantly come to see our small party on to the train. I could tell Charlotte was excited. She was planning to make one or two small purchases – a *chemise*, perhaps, or a spray of silk flowers – and see if any evening-gown designs caught her fancy. I was looking forward to seeing the new premises and perhaps confiding something of recent developments to Mrs Thompson during my fitting. Such modest hopes, to be so bitterly disappointed!

We disembarked from the train and managed to squeeze into a hansom cab with Beth in the middle for the journey to 'Madame Angeline', as the establishment is now called. Arriving at a white stucco building, we were shown by the doorman into a large reception room divided up by pillars and dotted about with the sort of furniture one might find in any elegant drawing room: sofas, chairs and side tables bearing vases of flowers. It was all most refined. The walls were painted soft grey, a fire burned in the grate and a maid bustled between the various groups of clients bearing a tray of refreshments. We hadn't been gazing about for longer than a minute or so before Miss Pratt appeared, smiling toothily, to guide us to our own apportioned area of the room with the offer of a cup of tea and the assurance an assistant would soon be with us. It was hard to believe the business could have changed so much in little more than a month. Mrs Thompson – or Madame Angeline, as perhaps we should now call her – is clearly going from strength to strength.

There was no sign of the lady herself, although there were constant comings and goings as parties were led towards, or appeared from, side doors which presumably led to fitting rooms. Charlotte leant towards me, panic written all over her face, and hissed, 'Not really our sort of place, is it?' I began to wish she hadn't come; I could have pulled it off on my own. Before long our *vendeuse*, Miss Hemmings, appeared to take me away for my fitting. She and I were walking towards one of the side rooms when out of the blue, suddenly the blow fell. We came face to face with Mrs Thompson herself, shepherding none other than – Araminta, and her mother, the Countess! A glowing, happy Araminta in a gown of sky-blue ondoline, flushed with success. How well I remember that feeling.

The Countess smiled at me distantly and

inclined her head a little before sweeping past. We've only met a couple of times and I've always found her a forbidding figure. Araminta, however, was more forthcoming. 'Eugenie!' she cried, sweeping me into an awkward embrace. 'What a delightful surprise.' As though I were the last person she expected to see at Madame Angeline's.

'Oh, Mrs Thompson and I are old friends,' I replied when I'd disengaged myself. 'I had no idea you knew her too.'

'Well, of course,' she said. 'We wouldn't have dreamed of announcing my engagement until we knew Angela could design the wedding gown.' (Angela!) She gave a theatrical start and added, 'Whoops! Now the cat is out of the bag. Well, it will be in *The Times* next week and anyway you should be one of the first to know. In fact everything was arranged some time ago but we couldn't make it public, for reasons you'll understand.'

So there we have it. She is engaged to be married to Lawrence somebody or other, just as soon as decently possible now the requisite year of mourning for her brother is over. No title apparently, but of course as an earl's daughter she'll still be known as Lady Araminta. I suppose she and her husband will live at Brixham Abbey, which I once thought would be my home, and it will be their son who inherits the title, rather than mine and Freddie's. Of course I was glad to see her looking so well but it is certainly a bitter pill to swallow. I managed to conceal my feelings, however, and congratulated her fulsomely; nobody could have guessed the pang in my heart.

'And how are you, my dear friend?' Araminta asked, composing her features into an expression of sympathy. 'Still putting up a brave front, I see. I do *so* admire your spirit.'

'As a matter of fact I shall shortly have happy news of my own to announce,' I heard myself say. 'Along the same lines as yours, although the details have not yet been finalized so please don't breathe a word to anyone.'

'How exciting! My lips are sealed,' she said, raising a finger theatrically to them. 'But let me be the very first to wish you well, dear Eugenie.' We embraced again. Afterwards she held me at arms' length and, gazing sorrowfully into my face, sighed, 'Life goes on, as it needs must. Darling Freddie. Gone but not forgotten.' And on that note, she bade me farewell. Mrs Thompson smiled and pressed my hand, murmuring that she would see me later, before whisking Araminta away to rejoin her mother who was sailing majestically towards the door.

I followed Miss Hemmings mechanically into the fitting room where my ballgown was waiting and allowed myself to be helped into it. Miss Hemmings, clearly worried by my lack of enthusiasm, assured me the white satin and I were ravishing. Objectively

Eugenie's Story

I had to agree but inside, I was still trying to digest the implications of what I had just told Araminta.

And then Mrs Thompson was at my side. 'Marvellous news!' she breathed discreetly into my ear. 'No one deserves happiness more than you, Miss Vye. Don't be downcast. I'm sure any little difficulties will soon be ironed out.'

'Nobody else knows, not even my family,' I said. 'Please keep this a secret, won't you, Mrs Thompson?'

'But of course!' she assured me. 'I am the very soul of discretion. We shall save all talk of wedding gowns or trousseaux until a later date, entirely at your convenience, and I shall be the picture of surprise when your engagement is announced.'

I managed to smile. After all, it can't be long before either Mr Hamilton-Greene or Lord McGillie asks me to marry him. A vision of them both gazing at me at the Hunt Ball as I whirled past in this exquisite ballgown flashed into my head. Perhaps I should dance with Henry Duxford all evening to make them jealous. 'That's better,' Mrs Thompson said. 'Nobody who looks so beautiful should be anything but happy. There! Perfection. I don't think a single alteration's required. Now if you'll forgive me, Miss Vye, I must take my leave.'

'Just a minute, Mrs Thompson,' I heard myself say. 'I should like to order a couple more things – something to wear to the theatre and a reception gown, perhaps – and have a look at your robes and *peignoirs*. May we make another appointment? In a week or so I'll be up in London for the season.'

If I'm soon to be married, I must have suitable clothes. Somehow or other the bill will be settled. Papa must agree when he sees how important this is or, as Mrs Thompson hinted, a gentleman may step into the breach. Her business is clearly prospering so she won't mind waiting a month or two if necessary; I know Mama often takes an age to settle her bills. At any rate she seemed delighted by my request and pressed my hand again briefly, saying Miss Hemmings would make the necessary arrangements, before hurrying away.

I rejoined Charlotte, trying to subdue my tumultuous feelings while we discussed wreaths, wraps and silk roses. There was no point mentioning my encounter with Araminta as they hardly know each other. Miss Hemmings was most ingratiating but Charlotte could only bring herself to order a parasol; perhaps she'll pluck up the courage to return to Madame Angeline with her mother. You can take a horse to water but you can't make it drink, as Nanny Roberts used to say. Well, I've done what I can for Charlotte. Now I must look after myself.

*

I've hardly slept all night. The grief of losing Freddie has returned. I've tried to practise forbearance but it's too hard to see Araminta resplendent with the joy that should have been mine, and no acknowledgement of the ties that once bound us. A year ago I was part of that family and now I'm nothing to them – cast aside with barely a glance. 'One of the first to know,' indeed! And then only by virtue of a chance meeting. I couldn't bear the pitying way in which Araminta looked at me, so full of sympathetic condescension. That was why I said what I did. It's not so very far from the truth, anyway. However now the pressure to find a suitable fiancé sooner rather than later is redoubled. Araminta is bound to talk and I'm not sure Mrs Thompson is quite as discreet as she claims; seeing the number of ladies in her new establishment has made me realize the reach of her influence. Madame Angeline's is certainly a very elegant place but I found myself missing the personal service Mrs Thompson offered in her little house behind Oxford Street, and regretted having confided in her at all.

My only consolation is that Rory arrived yesterday. He had called at the Dower House and so wasn't at home when we returned from the station, but had returned to the Hall in time for dinner. Sometimes I think he understands me better than anyone. If the occasion presents itself, I've decided to tell him about Mr Hamilton-Greene and ask his advice. Confiding my thoughts in this diary is all very well but it's rather a one-sided process; I feel in need of some loving guidance.

When Beth has finished her ministrations I shall take a light breakfast in my room before church. He must be there today, surely – it's Easter Sunday, when everyone gathers to celebrate the rising of our Lord. I'm wearing a demure brown holland gown with green satin sleeves and bands of green satin at the waist, and fixing my mind on higher things.

Eugenie's Story

Tuesday April 4th

All is well in my world once again. We understand each other, and the first steps have been taken along a road that leads ... where, I wonder? To a castle in Ireland, perhaps, overlooking the rushing Boyne. I can see myself there and a new life unfolding with him at my side: a life in which I am free and happy at last. What unexpected chances Fate throws in one's path! How vital it is to seize them before they disappear!

To church on Sunday and there he was, not presuming to sit in the family pew this time but mingling in an unassuming manner with the rest of the congregation. I wore a delicious Easter bonnet trimmed with flowers and a small stuffed robin, wings outstretched, mounted most realistically on a spring so it appears to move along with me. Afterwards he joined our party and was introduced to Rory by Edward, who clearly thinks most highly of him. Mr HG told us (with a particular glance at me) that he'd had to spend some time in London, which had prevented him from calling. In answer to my tactful questions, he went on to share some information about the business he and Edward have embarked upon together. Apparently his stable-owning cousin recently came across a truly outstanding gelding: 'the finest piece of horseflesh you ever set eyes on.' A consortium was quickly established to buy the animal, in which Edward has participated, and they had just received news it had won its first race by a furlong. 'Only a county steeplechase, but it's the start of great things.'

Edward looked most gratified. 'I told you this was a good investment!' he said to Kate. 'You'll be able to fund those precious poorhouses out of the proceeds.' She clearly wasn't pleased to hear her project referred to in this way and, sad to say, it seems the closeness between herself and Edward brought about by the accident may be only temporary. He went on to suggest that HG might come to luncheon with us at Swallowcliffe the next day, when an informal picnic at the boathouse had been planned. Mama readily agreed, which surprised me as she is usually inflexible where social occasions are concerned. Yet Mr Hamilton-Greene has won us all over (apart from Kate, perhaps) and my heart leapt to see him treated as an honorary member of the family. The knowledge we were soon to meet again made the pain of parting a little easier to bear.

Spent the afternoon trying to ride a bicycle under Harriet's instruction. Bicycling would be one way for me to gain a little freedom but it's a difficult skill to master and Harriet isn't the most patient of teachers. Papa has bought a small bicycle for John, who has taken to it like a duck to water and insisted on circling around me, whooping loudly with excitement, which was most off-putting. Also I refuse to wear those hideous bloomers Harriet and Miss Habershon go in for, and my skirts kept catching on the chain. After dinner we played parlour games until midnight. The house is so full of fun when Rory's home!

At last to bed where I fell asleep thinking about a certain person: his eyes, his voice, the set of his shoulders. That night I dreamed he and I were in a boat, far out to sea. We stood close together at the rail, looking down into the clear water where a shoal of silvery fish swirled about together, before a sudden shock sent them darting away in all directions like flickering splinters of light.

When I appeared for breakfast the next morning, Rory was in the dining room, reading *The Times*. 'I bumped into Araminta FitzWilliam the other day,' I said lightly. 'Apparently she's engaged. Don't suppose there's any announcement yet?'

Much rifling of the pages ensued. 'Oh yes, here we are,' he reported. 'She's snaffled the Honourable Lawrence Fishburne.' When I asked whether we knew the Fishburnes, he said yes we did: they have a villa near Margate and Lady F breeds goats. 'You mustn't worry so much about getting married, sis,' he added, *à propos* of nothing. 'You're a lovely girl – it's bound to happen sooner or later. There's no rush. You've had a simply horrid time, losing Freddie like that. Perhaps you should lie low for a while longer until you've completely recovered.'

I told him about India but he only chuckled

and said Mama couldn't have been serious, which shows how much he knows about the situation. It's all very well for men: they can afford to loiter about for years and they only become more desirable, not less. Take Lord McGillie, who must be thirty-five if he's a day. 'The main thing is not to look desperate,' Rory went on. 'Pretend it's a game, like the charades we were playing last night.'

'I'm trying,' I said. 'But it isn't really a game, is it? It's the most important decision I shall ever make. And the more time I spend pretending, the harder it is to know how I truly feel. Sometimes I hardly recognize myself.'

'Oh, you'll know when it's the real thing,' he said, tossing the newspaper aside and looking at me seriously for once. 'And that's the time to lay your cards on the table. Don't spend the rest of your life regretting what you let slip through your fingers.'

I was just about to tell him that in fact the real thing *had* come along when, with her usual immaculate timing, Mama entered the room and I had to return to my poached egg. Beneath my quiet demeanour, however, tumultuous thoughts were whirling. How extraordinary that Rory should have given me such appropriate advice! It was a remarkable conversation altogether because he and I never usually discuss affairs of the heart. He must have guessed what lay between Mr Hamilton-Greene and me and was giving us his tacit approval. One by one, the pieces of the puzzle are falling into place.

*

I thought carefully about how to dress for luncheon. It's so lovely down at the boathouse on a sunny day, all greeny gold and dappled shade. Waterlily flowers burst from the flat green discs of their leaves and willow fronds sway in the quiet water, disturbed only by whirring dragonflies and the occasional plink of a fish leaping up to catch a fly. One may even spot the iridescent flash of a kingfisher, flitting from branch to branch among the overhanging trees.

I was tempted to wear my teagown but it's not particularly practical for clambering in and out of boats, so in the end I settled for a blue frock with my green Eton jacket (watery shades, like those smudgy Impressionist paintings), and a green hat trimmed with daisies. 'Blue and green should never be seen, without another colour in between,' goes the saying, but the jacket has white lapels. Besides, in my opinion rules were made to be broken. I've always been a pioneer in that respect.

We assembled in the drawing room to wait for our guests: John fidgeting with impatience, Harriet stuffing her notebook and specimen bottles into a satchel, Rory watching out of the window for the Dower House party, jingling coins in his pockets, Papa morose at the thought of having to make conversation and Mama self-contained as usual. Yet

I've noticed she seems happier when John's home. Her eyes soften when she looks at him, and I hear her running upstairs to the nursery to say goodnight to him every evening. I suppose it's natural she should love him more than the rest of us – he's her own flesh and blood, after all, rather than a stepchild – but it's a pity she couldn't have summoned up a little more enthusiasm for us when we were small. Nanny Roberts was the closest thing to a mother in our lives, and she had her limitations.

I occupied myself with *The Lady*. Sir Walter Prendergast lies ill of typhoid fever in his residence at Henley-on-Thames; I saw his daughter once, riding a big bay horse down Rotten Row with her elbows sticking out. The dates of the May drawing-rooms have not yet been fixed by the Queen, who is still in Italy, and a son and heir has been born to the Duke of Portland.

And then at last the wait was over, and they were there. Every time I see him, I wonder if the magic will still be there, and every time he reassures me with thrilling glances and meaningful remarks (as meaningful as they can be, given the presence of others) that it is. The servants had already taken a dog-cart loaded with provisions and linen down to the boathouse. We followed in their wake, through the rose garden and across the lawn, and it came about quite naturally that he and I should end up walking together with John between us. He talked so naturally and kindly to my inquisitive little brother that I was beguiled all the more, and when John demanded that we should swing him between us, each taking one of his hands, I was perfectly happy to agree. Mr Hamilton-Greene smiled at me over John's head and my heart sang with happiness. We might as well have been holding hands ourselves – and actually an intermediary was better since I didn't have to worry about eczema (gloves notwithstanding). The only blot on the horizon was Mama following close behind, listening to our every word. However I told myself not to be cowed and, laughing merrily, lifted John into the air again.

Luncheon was laid out ready for us on the boathouse veranda, overlooking the water: the usual spread of cold roast beef, veal-and-ham pie, baskets of salad and bread, various cheeses, stewed fruit in corked glass bottles, biscuits and plum cake. I sat next to John and occupied myself putting tempting morsels on his plate, spoiling him while I can. He seems very young still to be away from home but there we are; no doubt school will toughen him up. At first the conversation was desultory. Rory, Papa and Edward talked about restoring the old shooting lodge in the middle of Monks' Wood, and Mama asked after Kate's cousin and aunt, whose boat was presently docking in Liverpool. Only when our chatter was all but exhausted did Mr Hamilton-Greene presume to regale us with tales of old Ireland:

myths and legends that must have been told around peat fires from one generation to the next. The famous white trout, for example, who turned into a beautiful young woman when fried in a pan, and the underground springs that confer the blessing (or is it a curse?) of eternal life on all those who drink from them. I could have listened until night fell, and it must have been an hour or so at least before John became restless and Rory and Papa took him off for a walk with the dogs.

'Listen to me blathering on,' Mr HG said, jumping to his feet and offering a turn around the lake in the rowing boat to any interested parties. I was about to accept when Mama said she would find that most diverting and rose to her feet, unfurling her parasol. I don't think I've ever seen her boating before. Being a married woman, of course she has no need of a chaperone, but I thought her behaviour unfitting for someone her age: laughing and reclining in such an undignified manner. One might almost accuse her of sprawling. I felt embarrassed on her behalf, especially since I knew full well Mr HG had meant the invitation for me and was only issuing it to the company in general out of politeness. Eventually my turn came, with Harriet agreeing to accompany us. She sat in the stern of the boat, I took my place in the prow, like Cleopatra sailing down the Nile on her gilded throne, and he sat facing me over the oars in the middle seat. His strong arms in shirtsleeves,

Eugenie's Story

dancing sunbeams reflected from the water, the rhythmic splash of oars as we glided through a carpet of waterlilies – all combined to induce in me a state of near-swooning bliss. Harriet was fishing out samples of pondweed and paid us no attention; we might as well have been alone.

Mr HG apologized for boring me with his 'auld stories' but I begged him to continue as I found them fascinating. What a conversation it was! He told me all about Meath, that lush green county where the High Kings of Ireland made their seat in ancient times. The countryside is beautiful in the dog days of summer but it is in winter that the place comes alive apparently, as everyone lives for hunting. 'You'd love it there,' he said, pulling back on the oars, 'a grand rider like yourself. But there's not much in the way of entertainment such as theatre and shopping.'

'Oh, I don't care much for those amusements,' I assured him, my heart pounding. 'The social whirl can be so exhausting.'

The more I think about it, the truer these words ring. The whole season long, all we do is race from one engagement to another: talking, talking, talking. But what do we actually say? Isn't a quiet life beside the person one loves, the only person in the world who really matters, the ideal to which one should aspire? I believe if I were with him, I'd happily abandon the opera for good.

'Then we understand one another very well,'

he said, with such a radiant smile I had to look away, dazzled. 'Sure but you'll have to come visit one day and I can show you around. You'd be the belle of the ball.'

I can't write any more – my heart is too full. Except to say that as he gave me his hand to disembark at the end of our excursion, he asked me in a low, urgent voice to save him the last dance at the Hunt Ball, and I agreed.

I have a sense of impending destiny. Only three more days to go. 'The moving finger writes, and having writ, moves on,' as the poet says. Or something similar.

Eugenie's Story

Wednesday April 5th

Nerves increasing but trying to maintain an air of calm. To the Dower House for tea today, to meet Kate's relations. Seized with trepidation at the last minute: these American girls are so smart and everybody likes to hear their accent, no matter what they actually have to say. However as soon as I saw Miss Johnson, the cousin, I was reassured. She has a pleasant face and a friendly smile but she's no great beauty. In fact she reminds me of Roger, Harriet's lop-eared rabbit that used to amble round the schoolroom. She has the same sandy-coloured hair, which she wears coiled in loops over her ears, small brown eyes and hopeful expression. The extraordinary thing is, in conversation we found out her birthday is the same day as mine! She is exactly a year younger than I.

'That means we're bound to be friends, don't you think?' she said, clutching on to my hand. (Why must people do that?) I felt like offering her a carrot. Her mother, Aunt Jane, or Mrs Johnson to us, holds forth loudly on any topic one cares to name; if she went head to head with Lady Duxford I'm not sure who would win. They are both well-dressed, albeit a little showily – daughter in red-and-white *foulard*, mother in pale yellow satin – and most impressed by the Dower House and everything English. I suppose Miss Johnson is on the hunt for a husband and hoping Kate will introduce her to some eligible young men. Well, good luck is all I can say.

Miss Johnson loves my teagown and I've promised to take her to Madame Angeline's. Both she and her mother are trembling with excitement over the Hunt Ball and so am I, though managing to conceal it, I think. I haven't seen any more of Mr Hamilton-Greene but he is constantly in my thoughts. I feel certain he is going to propose. Could I really leave my home and family to live in another country? And what sort of life would it be? I've heard the Dublin season is delightfully jolly and surely a person as convivial as Mr HG would want to sample some of its delights, no matter what he says about the quietness of the place. I must try to find out more about this castle of his, too. A certain amount of dilapidation is picturesque but damp is bad for the bones.

Two days to go.

Thursday April 6th

I had no idea when laying down my pen yesterday that I was shortly to embark on one of the most thrilling experiences of my life. Perhaps it was just as well, otherwise I should never have gone to sleep at all. Yet sleep I did, only to be awakened some time later by bright moonlight seeping into my room through a crack in the curtains, and the noise of horses' hooves outside. Who on earth could be about at that hour? Seizing a wrap from the end of my bed, I threw it around me and went to the window, my hair tumbling about my shoulders. A dark figure was riding along the terrace towards the stables, leading a second horse by the reins. I instantly recognized the face that turned to look in my direction, no doubt attracted by the movement. Throwing up the window, I called softly, 'Yoo hoo, Mr Hamilton-Greene! What are you up to?' It was just as well I'd heard the horses or he might have spent all night trying to work out which window opened on to my room.

'Miss Vye!' He pretended to be surprised, and for a moment did truly seem lost for words.

I put him out of his misery by asking, 'Are we to go riding again?'

'Sure and why not,' he hissed, going along with the pretence this was my idea. 'It's a glorious night, and the moon too bright for sleeping.'

I hesitated for a moment. What if someone else had been woken by the noise and saw us? Yet the appeal was irresistible and I knew if I turned it down, I should regret my lack of courage for ever. Thank goodness I wear a corset at night! I couldn't get into my Busvine habit without Beth's help but managed to slip on a suitable skirt and cape, and tying back my hair as best I could, hurried downstairs on gossamer feet.

'You have brought me Mama's horse,' I whispered when we were together. 'How did you get her out of the stable and saddled up?' Bella can be a little temperamental for anyone but my stepmother.

'Oh, I slipped the stable lad a shilling,' he said with a grin. 'Now let's be off quick before anyone catches us.'

Never, ever will I forget that wonderful ride: Mr Hamilton-Greene ahead of me on Papa's hunter, turning back occasionally to check I was following as we pounded through the shadowy fields, lit so eerily by the moon and empty but for the occasional flash of a rabbit's tail, or the dark outline of a fox slipping into the shelter of a copse. At one point I saw a ghostly white shape hanging on the air ahead of us and felt my heart pound with fear, until its rasping call announced this was only a barn owl out hunting. Bella was tiring, however, and eventually we had to turn the horses for home. Oddly enough she had been flecked with sweat as we set off, but Mr Hamilton-Greene explained he had already taken her for a quick turn, worried she might be too fresh for me to handle. He really is the height of consideration.

'I didn't think you'd come on a jaunt like this,' he said as we trotted back. 'A proper young lady like yourself.'

'Oh, I have my moments,' I replied. Indeed just then I felt myself invincible, flushed with the night, and the moonlight, and the wild gallop. I hardly cared that anyone might see us, even Mama herself; although she doesn't like anyone else to ride Bella

Eugenie's Story

(not that Mr Hamilton-Greene would know that) and it would have been difficult to explain.

All too soon we were back at the Hall – but only just in time, for the birds were beginning to sing their morning song and the first light of dawn was streaking the horizon. The servants would soon be up and about. I jumped down and Mr HG dismounted too. 'I'll take the horses back,' he whispered. 'Goodbye, Miss Vye. You're a grand girl. Don't let anyone tell you different.'

And then he kissed me. Yes, he bent his head and kissed me on the cheek!

'Wait,' I managed to stammer as he turned to go. 'I shall see you at the Hunt Ball, shan't I?' The final note in his farewell had alarmed me.

'I hope so,' he said, 'but I can't be certain. There's some business come up at home which might delay me.'

'Then when shall I see you next?' I asked, my voice breaking into an unseemly croak. 'We are shortly going up to London for the season.'

'I'll come back for you,' he promised.

'We shall be at Number 39, Bedford Square,' I said. 'My brother and sister-in-law are staying there too. We're taking the house together.'

'Don't worry, I'll find you,' he said. 'Another fine night we'll go riding again in the moonlight, Miss Vye, if you'll come down to meet me.'

'I will,' I breathed, watching him go, 'I most

certainly will!'

The noise of horses' hooves sounded dangerously loud but at last the little party had disappeared from view without seeming to attract attention. Hurrying through a back door and upstairs, I pulled off my outer garments as quickly as I had put them on, fell into bed and sank almost immediately into a deep sleep. Had I dreamed the whole episode? I wondered upon waking some hours later. Beth had already tidied away my clothes, but traces of mud at the hem of my skirt brought the adventure back to me so vividly that I blushed to the roots of my hair and put a hand to my cheek where he had kissed me.

Oh, the touch of his lips! I can feel it still.

*

The rest of the morning and luncheon passed somehow. I worried lest Mama should notice my distracted mood but she seemed wrapped up in her own thoughts. And then to add to the air of unreality, this afternoon we were honoured by a visit from Lord McGillie and his aunt. He seems much the same after his trip abroad, only perhaps a little redder in the face. I found myself considering him dispassionately. There's no doubt he's what my stepmother would term 'a catch'. Monkton Abbey is by all accounts a very grand residence on the shores of Loch Tarbert – Connie stayed there once, I believe

– and they also have a house in Carlton Terrace. But oh, his manner is verging on the insufferable! He has the most disconcerting habit of fixing his eyes on a point somewhere above one's head while he talks: almost exclusively about himself, in an accent I find hard to decipher and unattractive (unlike a certain person's!). If the family wasn't so illustrious, one might accuse him of trying to appear 'refined'. His aunt is a timid little thing with a hearing trumpet.

Miss Johnson and her mother happened to call while he was there. They seemed overawed by Swallowcliffe and Mama as its stately *châtelaine*, and I was concerned lest meeting a member of the Scottish aristocracy overwhelm them completely. They rose valiantly to the occasion, though it soon became obvious they could hardly understand a thing His Lordship said. He spent a great deal of time explaining the spawning season of salmon in the Tay, which left us all at a loss for words. At last Mrs Johnson remarked she thought afternoon tea a wonderful British tradition – something of a stab in the dark but at least it steered us into safer waters, conversationally speaking, and sparked a discussion about the merits of Eccles cakes to which everyone could contribute. We breathed a sigh of relief when Lord M finally made his indecipherable farewells and departed, aunt in tow. While Mama entertained Mrs Johnson in the drawing room, I showed Miss Johnson something of the house. I think we *are* going to be friends: her innocence and enthusiasm are charming.

When all our visitors had left, Mama informed me I ought to have paid Lord M more attention. 'You're not in a position to treat him so cavalierly,' she said tartly. 'If you're not careful, one of these American girls will snap him up. Still, he certainly seems struck with you at the moment.'

What would she think of Mr Hamilton-Greene as a suitor? Not a great deal, undoubtedly. It's true my life would be a great deal easier in practical terms were I to become Lady McGillie and the Countess of Tarbert in due course, with a wardrobe of new gowns to boot. However I don't think I could bear to be married to Lord M even for that. Imagine those long winter evenings, the mist rolling in across the loch and Himself, muttering away on the other side of the fireplace! Having galloped with Mr HG under the moonlight, how could I possibly settle for such an existence? I am destined for greater things.

I am tormented by the thought he might not be able to attend the Hunt Ball and will somehow be prevented from visiting us in London. 'I'll come back for you,' I can hear him saying. But when, O Lord, when?

Only one more day to go.

Eugenie's Story

Saturday April 8th

I'm trying hard to maintain an even keel but it's not easy. Everything is up in the air; I am contemplating momentous change and must continue my careful record of events for posterity.

So: yesterday morning, the day of the Hunt Ball. (Only yesterday? It seems a lifetime ago.) I breakfast quietly in my room on grapefruit and black coffee. Downstairs I find not one but two florists' boxes addressed to me, one containing a bouquet of red roses wrapped in tissue paper and the other a bunch of white gardenias – and no card with either! One I assume is from Mr HG and the other from Lord McGillie, but which is which? Eventually I hit on the idea of taking a bouquet made from both flowers to the ball, thus avoiding causing offence to either gentleman. I read Montaigne's essays in the drawing room as a calming measure (only moderately effective) until our house guests arrive. Mama has asked a couple of friends from her set – the Harpies, I call them collectively, as they're always peering over their fans and muttering – Lady Faulkner and Mrs Nash with her daughter, who has come out this season. Aunt Georgina and a scattering of second and third cousins have been invited too, along with Plum, who never misses the occasion. There's much laughter and chat over luncheon, to which Kate and Edward and the Americans have been invited. Mrs Nash's daughter, Beatrice, is painfully shy and I do my best to put her at ease. In the afternoon we play croquet and tennis or stroll about the gardens.

As the evening draws nearer, my nerves increase. I retire to my room after tea, earning a frown from Mama for this lack of sociability. No matter; I need time alone to prepare myself for what is to come. I spend a long time in the bath, rehearsing – and yes, I must be honest enough to admit this – various conversations between myself and both HG and Lord McGillie. The important thing is not to be taken unawares. In due course Beth helps me into my stays, petticoats, the dazzling ballgown and a new pair of kid gloves. She combs, coils and pins my hair, tucks rosebuds and gardenias into the sash at my waist, and at last I'm ready. I pinch my cheeks which are deathly pale.

We arrive at Fountains Court around ten o'clock; the ballroom is already full. I see many familiar faces amid the throng – the Duxfords, Letty Morgan and her mother, Millicent Shoosmith, the Giffords, Lord McGillie – but no sign of him, the one person whose presence is vital. Where can he be? My dance card begins to fill. I do my best to appear calm, inclining my head gracefully towards each gentleman whose hand I take in the quadrille. Candles burn lower in the huge candelabra; when Lord McGillie claims me for a waltz, the shoulders of his tailcoat are splashed with wax. He's danced with Beatrice Nash, Julia Johnson and Charlotte

Eugenie's Story

Duxford, among others, and is beginning to perspire. Rory also dances with Charlotte, who can't take her eyes off him. Poor girl: her feelings are so transparent. I take the floor twice with Henry and sit out a turn with George Gifford, who tells me about his recent golfing holiday in Broadstairs. I listen with half an ear, keeping my eye on the door.

When it's time for supper, Lord McGillie advances purposefully towards me. Mama shoots me one of her commanding looks so I bow to the inevitable and take Lord M's arm, composing my features into a smile. Mama gives an approving nod, though she wouldn't be so pleased if she could read my thoughts. Every sinew is straining away from my lugubrious companion. He thanks me for wearing his gardenias; I collect myself in time to thank him for sending them. So Mr HG must be responsible for the roses. Henry offers his arm to little Beatrice Nash, who accepts thankfully and giggles at some remark he whispers in her ear.

Over supper, Lord M tucks away a large quantity of creamed chicken, telling me more about the correct flies for catching trout than I could ever wish to know. Suddenly I can't bear his presence a second longer and rise to my feet, murmuring something about feeling faint before hurrying from the room. A stream of cool air beckons from French windows thrown open in the empty ballroom, where a solitary violinist is tuning his instrument. I slip out on to the terrace and into the blessed cover of darkness, escaping at last from the prying eyes of matrons, chaperones, suitors, rivals. There are one or two couples strolling about so I pause, fanning myself and trying to look purposeful. Eventually I seize my moment, flit across the terrace like a wraith and down a flight of steps to the garden below. I perch on a stone bench for a moment in my rustling white satin gown, like a great stranded seabird, trying to regain some measure of calm. Why is Mr Hamilton-Greene not here? What business could have detained him?

Eventually solitude and fresh air work their magic. My breathing gradually slows and peace descends. So does rational thought: I mustn't be seen out here alone. I realize the peril of my situation and shrink back into the shadows at the sudden sound of footsteps crunching along the gravelled terrace above, accompanied by the whiff of cigar smoke. To my dismay, a familiar voice cuts sharply through the night: it's Kate, although I've never heard her so angry. She's arguing with my brother. They must have stopped directly above my head because I can hear every word although they're not talking loudly. To the best of my memory, this is how the conversation goes.

KATE: I can't believe you could have been so foolish! Handing over such a large sum of money to a man you only met a couple of weeks ago – in

return for what, exactly? We don't even know this mythical racehorse exists.
EDWARD: Yes we do. I've seen the papers and a photograph. Anyway, Mr Hamilton-Greene is a thoroughly decent chap – you of all people should know that – and a friend of the Duke's besides.
KATE: Well, if he's such a decent chap, why has he disappeared so suddenly without leaving any address? He's got the gift of the gab all right but I don't trust him or this mysterious cousin. He's probably just another invention along with the horse. The long and short of it is, the man's scarpered with a great deal of money and we haven't a clue where he is.
EDWARD: Don't meddle in what you don't understand. Financial decisions are my concern not yours.
KATE: Even though it's my money you're risking?
EDWARD: What do you mean, *your* money? What was yours is now mine and I won't be questioned about what I do with it, least of all by my wife. I'm thinking of increasing my stake in this consortium, not reducing it. Your aunt certainly seems interested.
KATE: You've approached her for money? How dare you! Your behaviour is unforgiveable.

Eventually, thank goodness, Edward declares he's had enough of this and strides away. I hear his retreating footsteps, followed a few moments later by Kate's, and wait another ten minutes before climbing slowly back up to the terrace, trying to digest what I've heard. There must be some misunderstanding – I refuse to accept this picture of Mr Hamilton-Greene! Kate has been against him from the start for reasons I still don't understand. Perhaps she made advances towards him which he rejected, and is now lashing out through wounded pride? If there has been some problem with the horse, he has merely gone away to sort it out; that explains his absence, I'm sure. Yet I cannot say so without giving away more of my deepest feelings than I dare. It is an agonizing dilemma…

I return to the ballroom and stand trembling on the threshold for a moment before plunging back into the *mêlée*. Somehow I must hide my inner torment and smile, and nod, and force my feet to follow the age-old patterns. To add to my misery, Henry tells me in passing he sent the red roses; I find it hard to look grateful. I scratch out Mr Hamilton-Greene's name on my dance card and spend the last waltz skulking in the cloakroom with two other wallflowers, pretending to rub chalk marks off my gown. Rejoining the party, I see Beatrice Nash, flushed with all the excitement of her first ball, and feel about a hundred years old.

To compound the agony, in the carriage on the way home Mama tells me Lady Faulkner confided over ices she'd heard a rumour I had become secretly engaged. 'How on earth could such a ridiculous notion have got about? Just when I thought we were making progress! I hope nothing of this reaches Lord McGillie's ears or he'll drop you quicker than a hot potato.'

She has such a vulgar turn of phrase sometimes. 'Oh, you know how people talk,' I reply as evenly as possible. Beneath this calm exterior, however, my thoughts are racing and my heart is pounding thumpety-thump.

I cannot afford to panic but am perilously close to losing my head. We have just finished luncheon and I have come to my room to rest. I shall pray for sleep and at least temporary oblivion from my troubles.

Sunday April 9th

Things are both better and worse. Worse in that it appears Mr Hamilton-Greene has left behind an unpaid bill at The Greyhound. I take this to mean his absence is only temporary and he will soon return to settle it, but concede this could be used as further evidence against him. Better in that now I have an ally; in fact, two allies.

Yesterday afternoon Miss Johnson strolled over from the Dower House to pay us a visit. To be specific, to pay *me* a visit. We shared a cup of tea and chit-chatted with Mama before she suggested the two of us go for a stroll around the gardens to admire the daffodils, which carpet the ground in great drifts near the orangerie. As we contemplated the sunshine-yellow blooms, dancing gaily enough in the breeze to delight Wordsworth himself, she took my arm and said shyly, 'Miss Vye, I hope you don't mind me saying so but you looked a little anxious last night. I hope nothing has happened to upset you?'

Looking into her face, I saw no guile there, only sympathy and friendly concern. Somehow the whole story came spilling out: my *coup de foudre* on first meeting Mr Hamilton-Greene, the unfounded rumours that were circulating in his absence, and the assurances he gave me (though not the details of our night ride, which might have shocked her). 'He has returned temporarily to his native Ireland,' I said, 'but he promised to come back for me.'

'Oh, how romantic,' she sighed, with dreamy eyes. 'Mama and I have always wanted to visit the country, and even hoped we might fit in a trip before we go home. The Emerald Isle, land of the faery folk!'

'Perhaps one day you will come to visit us in the castle,' I said, allowing myself the luxury of a brief daydream. I also went on to tell her about my various difficulties with Mama, culminating in the threat of India or hydrotherapy, my unfortunate disclosure to Araminta in Mrs Thompson's hearing, and my outstanding bill at the dressmaker's, which has begun to weigh so heavily upon me – even, reaching further back into the past, my short-lived engagement to Freddie. Somehow I knew she wouldn't judge me and I was proved right. When at last I'd finished speaking, she murmured, patting my back, 'You poor girl. If that isn't the saddest thing I ever did hear. Well, no wonder.'

She understands; no wonder I sometimes give way to melancholy or seem a little strained. 'You mustn't keep all this to yourself,' she told me, her arm still tucked through mine as we walked towards a nearby bench. 'Will you let me be your friend, Miss Vye? You know I won't give away your secrets because I don't know anyone to tell them to, even if I had a mind. Oh, I just feel in my waters we're going to get along famously. Don't you think so?'

I could have cried, and in fact I had to wipe away

a few grateful tears at this unprompted kindness. It's as though Miss Johnson has been sent by Providence to help me in my hour of need. Perhaps I can return the favour with a few tactful hints about grooming and deportment, and possibly appropriate turns of speech when in polite company. We have agreed to call each other by our Christian names; I'm sure I can trust her completely.

So she is my first ally, and my second is no less welcome. He revealed himself to me later that same day. We had all been invited by the Duxfords to a musical evening with light refreshments: quite honestly the last occasion I felt like attending but I had agreed to play for Charlotte while she sang 'Woodman, Spare that Tree', and knew there would be a tremendous fuss if I let her down. (Not a song best suited to her voice, in my opinion, but she is quite fixed on it and performs with great emotion – which only Henry and I seem to find inappropriately directed towards forestry.)

Anyway I was ready in good time, having scarcely the heart to worry about my appearance, and descending the stairs when I heard a noise from the billiard room. Plum was there by himself, desultorily pocketing a few balls. I simply had to ask him whether he'd heard from Mr Hamilton-Greene, although I phrased the question as a casual enquiry. He told me he hadn't and a flicker of unease crossed his distinguished features; eventually he confessed

Eugenie's Story

to being deeply worried about having brought the young man to our house. Plum had bumped into Binky Braithwaite up in town and learned that, far from him being an old friend of Mr HG's, they had met for the first time earlier that evening. 'And now the fellow seems to have done a bunk,' he said, laying aside his cue and sinking disconsolately into a chair. 'I've settled his bill at The Greyhound but I've a dreadful feeling there may be further ramifications.'

I couldn't bring myself to reveal the conversation I'd overheard between Kate and my brother. 'Don't you trust Mr Hamilton-Greene at all?' I asked. 'He told me there was some business he had to settle and that's why he's gone away. He said he would come back and I'm sure he will.'

The Duke gave me a searching look. 'He hasn't ... taken advantage of you in any way?'

I assured him that was not the case, while feeling myself blush furiously at this half-truth. Plum seemed to accept my answer, although he said I must be sure to remember him if I ever needed any help or confidential advice. 'If only we knew where the young chap was!' he added. 'The longer he stays away with no explanation, the harder it is to account for his actions.'

This remark seemed to trigger some half-buried memory. 'Would you excuse me for a moment, Your Grace?' I asked, excitement rendering me strangely formal. 'There's something I've just remembered

I've forgotten – if you catch my drift.'

The vision had suddenly flashed into my mind of a folded scrap of paper, put away for safekeeping in my jewellery box: a receipt for horse feed and liniment, with a scribbled address in the top righthand corner which I had seen but not properly taken in at the time, what with all the confusion of Kate's accident. I ran upstairs and made straight for the box which stood in its usual place on my dressing table. Yes, there was the bill, and there was the address written upon it: 'P Green, Castle Mount, Dalkenny.' (I suppose 'Hamilton-Greene' might be something of a mouthful for a busy tradesman.) Mr HG had never told us the name of his village near Dublin but here it was in black and white. As I stared at the words, the outline of a most daring plan began to form in my mind. I could hear Julia saying, 'The Emerald Isle! Mother and I have always wanted to visit the country.' Well, why shouldn't the Johnsons and I go there together? Why not take matters into my own hands for once? The audaciousness of the idea set my pulse racing and my palms prickling with moisture but once it had entered my head, I couldn't think of anything else.

*

My rendition of 'Woodman, Spare that Tree' later in the evening was a little eccentric, I must confess, yet Charlotte and I received an enthusiastic round of applause as we drew to a triumphant close. I noticed Henry Duxford whisper something to Julia which made her laugh so much she had to leave the room; Lord McGillie, however, said he found our performance most affecting.

Tomorrow we leave for London. I am hoping desperately that word will soon come from Mr Hamilton-Greene but, if it does not, I have decided to find him and speak to him myself. Am I sufficiently brave to turn this impulse into action? Only time will tell...

London

Thursday April 13th

The only news of any importance is that Mr Hamilton-Greene has not called; nor have I received a message of any kind. I'm only half alive. Time passes as if in a dream. Every day I have been searching the streets that make up Bedford Square in case he has mistaken the number of our house, and watching the garden in the middle to see whether he might be waiting for me there. I look for his face in that of each passing stranger, dream of him every night. One day I run after a tall gentleman in the street who turns out to be a police constable. I instruct the butler to bring any letters directly to me and even apprehend the postman occasionally on our front steps. Nothing. The only post of any interest is an invitation to Araminta's wedding in June, at St George's Hanover Square; a little hasty but

Eugenie's Story

I suppose it has been planned in secret for months.

I've been too distracted to write my journal these past few days. In brief, this is the story thus far:

The setting: We are all a little on top of each other in Bedford Square as the party consists of Mama and (occasionally) Papa, Kate and Edward, the Johnsons, Aunt Georgina and myself – plus Beth, Agnes and Hortense, Papa's valet and the butler, housekeeper and cook with assorted maids and footmen. They can be heard clattering up and down the servants' staircase all day. The house was rather bare when we arrived but it has been made more presentable with rugs, tapestries and paintings sent up from Swallowcliffe besides the family silver, crystal and china. London is warm and dusty, the houses freshly painted and gay with window-boxes, the streets and parks filling up with friends and acquaintances in all their finery. I have no desire to talk to any of them.

The scenes: Firstly, a private view at the New Gallery. Terrifically crowded. Just as well nobody cares much about the paintings, apart from Julia and Henry Duxford who talk earnestly about Impressionism. According to Julia, various American painters are holed up in Parisian garrets, drinking absinthe as to the manner born.

What else? I take Julia to Madame Angeline's where she's received by Mrs Thompson herself and orders three gowns. I alight on a glorious shirt-waist in sky-blue chiffon, finished with gold net, chenille fringing and a *fichu* in French lace with a satin ribbon belt, and hear myself say I must have it, although my allowance is already exhausted and I haven't yet paid for the ballgown. What is one new blouse at a time like this? A drop in the ocean. The season is not yet in full swing but we go to the Haymarket to see the new play by Oscar Wilde (something of a disappointment), dine with the Galbraiths, the Morgans and many others, meet friends in Hyde Park after church and stroll about. Lord McGillie is much in evidence and we were invited to a supper party two days ago at his house in Carlton Terrace. I'm introduced to his mother, who examines me through her lorgnette. The house is dark and somewhat cluttered, crammed with furniture, knick-knacks and stuffed deer heads watching us mournfully from every wall. 'And we have died for *this?*' I seem to hear them asking. The other guests are a dull bunch so we do our best to entertain but Mrs Johnson holds forth for rather too long about a marvellous hotel just opened in New York, prompting the Countess to ask her neighbour loudly, 'Have you any idea what that odd little woman's talking about?'

Mama, loitering on the fringes of the Marlborough House set, has dined in the presence of the Prince of Wales. The Queen has returned from Italy and the engagement is announced between the Duke of York and lovely Princess May of Teck. (Aunt Georgina, who in rational moments has been predicting this for months, is quietly victorious.) We attend a ball at the Hotel Metropôle in aid of the Rest Home for Horses, and a Sale of Work at Cadogan House in aid of the Scottish Home Industries, where Mama buys a cashmere shawl. Mrs Black's Cottage Hospital Ball features a Hungarian band and a palmist, who tells me I shall soon be taking a journey across water in the company of a fair-haired stranger. She tells Julia the same, only her stranger is dark. Each night Julia and I sit up in her bedroom, talking over the day and the people we've met, and finding ourselves in perfect agreement. I don't think I've ever liked anyone quite as well as I like her. She has arrived just when I most need a friend, as spiteful tongues are already wagging behind my back. A hush falls when I enter the room, and I catch sly glances and hear stifled laughter behind fans. Encountering Araminta on Monday at the opera, she whispers, 'Don't give up! Surely any day now we shall be hearing happy news,' and I seem to see a malicious gleam in her eye as we part.

Mama is looking at me suspiciously too, although thankfully she has become distracted by Rory and a fellow officer who seem to be constantly at our house. As usual Aunt Georgina has only the haziest grasp of any given situation and notices nothing amiss, while Kate and Edward are so busy sniping at each other they have little energy left over for anyone else. Papa retreats to Swallowcliffe whenever possible and the Johnsons bustle about: shopping, chattering and marvelling at things. And that is our happy household.

I have tried to introduce the subject of Mr Hamilton-Greene so I can at least express my belief he's done nothing wrong, but no one wants to talk about him – least of all Kate and Edward. Edward would no doubt be furious to discover I have Mr HG's address, but I won't give it to him. I must resolve this matter by myself to have any chance of learning the truth.

My thoughts seesaw between direst foreboding and the conviction Mr HG is alone somewhere, struggling to put things right and too ashamed to write or call. I simply must let him know my feelings have not changed, that one person at least still has faith in him.

To that end, this evening I took Julia into my confidence, telling her of my determination to find my *amour* and speak to him directly, and suggesting that a sightseeing trip to Dublin – which she and her mother had been wanting to undertake anyway – would provide the ideal opportunity: killing two birds with one stone, so to speak. I was a little disappointed by her reaction, I must confess. 'Are you sure that's such a good idea?' she said. 'Wouldn't it be better to wait for him to come to you, or at least write? It doesn't seem quite respectable for us to chase after him.'

Eugenie's Story

'It seems all my life has been spent waiting for other people to act!' I burst out. 'I have to do something for myself at last. I know how Mr Hamilton-Greene will be feeling as he tries to resolve these difficulties. He probably considers himself unworthy of me, although I'm sure if anything has gone wrong with the investment it is through no fault of his. I must go to him, tell him all is not lost, and that I still have faith in him.'

'Well, I don't like keeping secrets from Mother,' she said.

'Oh, please help me, Julia!' I begged, clasping her hand and sinking to my knees. 'I have nobody else to turn to. Won't you be my friend in deed as well as word and help me?'

She muttered something about not wanting to lead me astray so finally I got up and said, a little stiffly, 'Well then, I shall take Beth and go alone. Please don't worry about me, all by myself in a strange country. I'm sure I can find my way.'

So she sighed, and hummed and hahed, and eventually said if I were set on going, we might as well turn it into a respectable expedition. She would ask her mother to accompany us on a short sightseeing tour of Dublin and the surrounding villages. 'I don't like to deceive her but it's not an actual lie,' she said. 'Perhaps we can arrange to visit this village and look around the castle. You shall have to act surprised when we bump into Mr Hamilton-

Greene, of course.'

'Thank you, my dearest friend,' I exclaimed, hugging her. 'It will be a wonderful journey of discovery for us all. I'm sure I shall be able to introduce you to all sorts of lovely people in Dublin.'

I think such an inducement may make Mrs Johnson more enthusiastic about the trip, and thus more likely to persuade Mama it's a good idea. Of course Mama would never have let me go alone and travelling by myself in secret would be unthinkable. With Julia beside me, however, all things are possible. I am shivering with anticipation and nerves, but resolute. To quote another favourite poem from my Commonplace book: 'I am the master of my fate, I am the captain of my soul'.

Saturday April 15th

Still no word from Mr HG. Mrs Johnson with her characteristic pioneering spirit is delighted by the idea of exploring the Emerald Isle, and Mama has given me permission to join the party. We leave on Wednesday. If we stay for a few days, we can be back in London before the season is in full swing – although of course our visit may be extended once Mr HG knows we are in the country.

Can I go through with this? I must; it's too late to turn back now. Hands plaguing me terribly.

Monday April 17th

Yesterday a party comprising Lord McGillie, Charlotte and Henry Duxford, Mama, the Johnsons, Plum and I, went to Richmond, to dine at The Star and Garter and thence take a boat down the river. Plum was looking particularly smart in a blazer and panama hat. I am suffering dreadfully from nerves at the moment but found myself reassured by the sight of him, so debonair and wise. During the course of the meal, Mrs Johnson revealed details of our sightseeing expedition and Plum immediately sent a searching glance across the table which set me blushing to the roots of my hair. Later, while we were deciding which boat to take, he drew me a little way aside and murmured, 'Has this forthcoming trip anything to do with a certain mutual friend of ours, or is your destination merely a coincidence?'

I reassured him with some non-committal reply

but he still seemed unconvinced. 'May I come with you?' he asked. 'I should hate to see your reputation compromised in any way.'

While it would be comforting to have a protector, I cannot risk the Duke becoming a member of our party. The only way I am going to find out the truth is by looking Mr Hamilton-Greene in the face and asking him for it. If he thinks there is anything like a lynch mob coming after him, he will take fright and disappear, no matter how little he may be to blame for what has happened. So I thanked Plum for his concern but said there was no need for him to accompany us. In the end he acquiesced, remarking Mrs Johnson seemed a sensible woman and he supposed she would look after me, and asking only for me to send word immediately should we run into any danger or difficulty in Ireland.

Out on the river, it was hard to continue the pretence of normality. Boating reminded me of that glorious afternoon on the lake at Swallowcliffe when Mr Hamilton-Greene had told me about life in Ireland: offering it up for my approval, or so it seemed. I was also a little nervous at the thought of the momentous course of action I was about to undertake. When Henry gave me his hand to disembark at Boulter's Lock, he said quietly, 'Is anything the matter, old thing? Hate to see you looking blue.'

'I'm perfectly all right, thank you,' I assured him

Eugenie's Story

hastily. It was unbearable to think of the Duxfords getting to hear of 'the Hamilton-Greene affair,' as Plum called it; I could imagine Lady D chewing over the details with gusto and Charlotte pretending to be shocked.

My spirits sank still further. I hardly noticed Lord McGillie had fallen into step beside me, and then that owing to his frantic pace we had become separated from the rest of the party. He was fairly trotting along the riverside path; I pictured him as a dot disappearing over the horizon with me trailing hopelessly in his wake, and couldn't help but smile. At which point he seized my hand and, contemplating the usual spot above my head, began to tell me about his father, who is currently unwell (from what I could make out). I tried to look sympathetic but why did he have to clutch at me with all the fervour of a drowning man, and what on earth was he talking about now? Eventually I caught a few phrases: 'taking advantage of the opportunity... conjunction of two noble families... approval from both sides...' and realized he was proposing. He seemed to add something about a struggle to the death, but surely I must have misheard. Unless perhaps it's the Tarbert family motto? On that unexpected note he dropped my hand abruptly and looked out at the river, where a couple of swans were gliding gracefully downstream.

So, there we are: I have my proposal. I can't say I was taken completely by surprise. I was able to thank him for according me such a great honour (at which he nodded solemnly), and ask whether he'd allow me a few days to think the matter over. He met my eyes at last and bowed, and together we watched the swans' stately progress while waiting for the others to catch up. They were swimming so contentedly side by side with their curving necks harmoniously aligned. I have heard it said that swans stay together for life. (Although I wonder how anyone can tell. Surely one swan looks very much like another?)

    I mulled over the alternatives during the course of the afternoon. Marrying Lord McGillie would solve all my problems: I would escape from Mama into a substantial home of my own, my good name in society would be restored, and my account at Madame Angeline's not only settled but extended. It doesn't seem fair to make use of His Lordship solely for the sake of expediency, but I might grow to like or at least respect him in due course. Besides, if rumours continue to circulate about me I might not receive another offer; certainly not such a respectable one. And yet... and yet...

    Julia was thrilled to hear I had received an offer of marriage. 'An abbey in Scotland!' she sighed, perching on the edge of my bed last night. (Staying in the same house allows us plenty of opportunity to chat.) 'How wonderful. And Lord McGillie is very ... knowledgeable, about all sorts of things. Are you sure you still want to go to Ireland? You know what they say: "A bird in the hand is worth two in the bush."'

I could imagine myself greeting guests in the lofty hall at Monkton Abbey, dressed in sables perhaps, with maybe a touch of the Tarbert tartan, a couple of deerhounds at my side. Yet try as I might to put Lord M into the picture, he simply wouldn't fit. There was only one person in my mind's eye.

'Don't you see, the need to go there is more urgent now than ever!' I told Julia. 'How could I accept another gentleman's proposal without talking to Mr Hamilton-Greene first? If he returned to find me engaged to another, it would surely break his heart.'

*

So the day after tomorrow we take the train from Euston to Holyhead and from there, a steamer across the Irish Sea. Beth is her usual recalcitrant self but I suppose that's to be expected. One might think she would express some gratitude at the prospect of a journey overseas and the chance to explore a new country, instead of going about with a face like thunder. I've a good mind to leave her behind and see how she likes that, but corsets don't lace themselves, more's the pity.

It is a daring expedition and the stakes are high. And although doubts beset me in the small hours, it's too late to turn back now.

Dublin

Wednesday April 19th
We have arrived! The journey has been exhausting but at last we're safely installed in the Shelbourne Hotel, overlooking St Stephen's Green with its small but picturesque lake where ducks are placidly floating. I've had enough of water to last me a lifetime, however – never have I felt as ill as I did this afternoon during that dreadful crossing. Poor Julia was similarly green about the gills, although she professes not to bear me any ill will for dragging her across the wild Irish Sea. Her mother spent the early part of the voyage on the ship's deck, despite the howling wind, apparently discussing Gladstone and his Home Rule Bill with a returning Irish landowner. Although the very thought of food turns my stomach, she's presently taking supper in the hotel dining room (probably making more new friends). She is indefatigable and in fact a reassuring presence.

Eugenie's Story

Now that we're here, only a few miles or so away from him, my nerves are very much on edge. My hands are bad and I'm hoping Beth has remembered to pack the Epsom Salts. Deciding what to bring was difficult without knowing what functions we might be attending, so I instructed her to prepare for all eventualities and we've brought a trunk plus several suitcases. We're planning to return on Saturday but our stay may of course be extended once Mr Hamilton-Greene knows we're here. I've written to Lord McGillie, promising to reply to his proposal as soon as we're back in London.

So, a short account of our journey: up at the crack of dawn to dress in a travelling costume of navy Scotch linen, to conceal smuts from the train, and neat straw hat secured with plenty of pins. Off to Euston by hansom cab, to be plunged into the throng of travellers coming and going: porters shouting, urchins dashing underfoot, paperboys calling, rough women hawking refreshments. Settle ourselves down in an empty carriage on the train, where we are unfortunately soon joined by a large red-faced gentleman who proceeds to suck pear drops during the entire journey. Julia and her mother are shocked by the state of the tenement housing we pass aboard our shrieking, rattling monster of a train, and the dreary slag heaps and mine-workings of northern England. By the time we arrive at Holyhead, fortified only by stale buns from the saloon car, we're all a little out of spirits. Then that dreadful sea crossing aboard a mail steamer to Kingstown Harbour, about which the less said, the better – only that finally it came to an end without inflicting any lasting damage – one more train ride, and we arrive at our hotel.

I've just left Julia's room after our usual nightly chat. She is still less than enthusiastic about the trip, and hasn't stopped fretting about concealing the truth from her mother. 'It's not too late, Genie,' she said. (That's what she calls me; I try not to mind.) 'You don't have to go through with this plan. We can stay here in Dublin and forget all about Dalkenny.'

'What would be the point of that?' I asked. 'We'd have made that awful journey just to go sightseeing. We can't give up now, not when the end is almost in sight.'

She still looked downcast, although that might have been due to her unflattering nightgown: no one with her complexion should ever wear pink, as I've already pointed out. I simply can't let her mood dampen my own. I'll need all the hope and courage I possess over the next few days if my dreams are to be realized; failure of nerve at this crucial point would be disastrous. And I need a friend, too.

'Come on, don't lose faith!' I urged. 'Your mother will think it's frightfully romantic if she ever finds out why we're really here. Why, she's like the nurse in *Romeo and Juliet*.'

Eugenie's Story

'And look how that ended up,' Julia replied gloomily.

Seeing she was quite determined upon melancholy, I wished her goodnight and went back to my own room, to write my journal for this momentous evening and then try to sleep. I cannot turn back now. To quote from Shakespeare again, 'Returning were as tedious as go o'er.' Although 'tedious' is not quite the right word.

Tomorrow we take the train to Drogheda and from there, a carriage to show us the local sights — including the castle at Dalkenny. Be still, my beating heart! I have set these plans in motion and must see them through.

Swallowcliffe Hall

Friday April 21st
I am undone. Things are not as I hoped, or imagined: I have been most wilfully and cruelly deceived. My life is ruined, quite possibly for ever. Julia and her mother are attending a ball at Dublin Castle – by invitation of the State Steward himself, no less, who turns out to be a cousin of the landowner Mrs Johnson met on the mail steamer – but I'm in no mood for dancing. My hands are in a shocking state. I wish I were dead.

Saturday April 22nd
This morning I groaned to find my eyes opening on another long day without hope, joy or affection. I should like to have passed away in my sleep but such a peaceful resolution is denied me; somehow this broken heart continues to beat. Tomorrow we take the boat back to Holyhead. Far from dreading the sea crossing, I welcome it: firstly for taking me away from this benighted country, and secondly for the opportunity it affords to end my torment. I was about to burn this journal but have decided to let it stand as a testimony to my suffering. The world will see what pain I had to endure, despite the best of motives and a pure and gentle soul. Truly, I am 'one who lov'd not wisely but too well'. Various individuals may have cause to rue their harsh words and cruel treatment meted out to me but by then it will be too late. That is their burden; I have chosen to lay mine down.

Eugenie's Story

Farewell to those I have known and loved, family and erstwhile friends. Eventually, I hope, you may remember me with a smile rather than bitter tears of regret.

London Again

Tuesday April 25th

Yet as you see, I could not do it: could not deliberately inflict such pain on others. My spirit may be wounded but a stubborn spark remains that refuses to be extinguished. I have chosen to live, to continue my journey in this cruel world. And a necessary stage of that journey is to look back and see where I have strayed from the path into brambles, potholes and vipers' nests. This is the first day I've felt able to write my journal in any detail. Agonizing as it must be to recall, here is an unvarnished account of the events that took place in County Meath: that most wretched of all godforsaken places, inhabited by sheep and inbred peasants in hovels which make the Beamishes' cottage seem like a palace.

  Casting back my mind, I see Julia, her mother and myself on the clackety line to Drogheda. We have left Beth at liberty to amuse herself in Dublin. She professes to have caught a cold on the sea crossing and goes about blowing her nose with a martyred expression: Joan of Arc could not look more long-suffering. Mrs Johnson is quizzing Julia on what we might find in these out-of-the-way villages and where we should take luncheon, which leads me to drop the name of Dalkenny and its castle into the conversation. I'm wearing the blue chiffon shirt-waist with a flounced black skirt and my rose-trimmed Leghorn hat, and am attracting much attention from the labourers and shop workers who are travelling with us on this rural train – although thankfully not in first class. Even here, however, there is an all-pervading smell of onions and the upholstery manages to be both threadbare and unpleasantly sticky. We have a carriage to ourselves. Beyond the grimy window, desolate fields punctuated by the occasional smallholding are visible through a fine drizzle; the countryside is miserably grey rather than lush green. I'm nervous, feeling suddenly a long way from home.

We arrive at Drogheda having crossed the famous viaduct (which sends Mrs Johnson into transports), and engage one of the less disreputable-looking carriages waiting at the railway station: a wagonette with a taciturn driver and two sway-backed horses. Beth managed to obtain a map of the area that morning so I've planned a route which, I've told the Johnsons, takes in some of the prettiest villages in the area, ending up at the castle in Dalkenny around mid-day. The coachman appears to understand my instructions, nods, puts an excuse for a hood over our heads and urges the horses into some sort of life. It's no longer raining as such but the very air seems dank, swollen with unshed raindrops. I feel my hair droop under the Leghorn hat, in sympathy with my spirits which have been up and down all morning and are currently down. Mrs Johnson chatters away about some relative whose great-grandmother might possibly have been Irish, or Scottish, or did she in fact come from Yorkshire? Far from being picturesque, the villages to which I have directed us are devoid of any interesting features whatsoever – except firstly, a group of women working in the fields, one with a baby strapped to her back, and secondly, an unfortunate simpleton who runs behind our carriage for half a mile or so, laughing and flapping his hands, until driven away by means of a well-aimed potato hurled by our driver. This does, however, achieve the near-impossible feat of stunning Mrs Johnson into silence.

After an hour or so, we arrive at yet another nondescript hamlet which an enamelled sign announces to be Dalkenny. We drive past a few miserable houses and a tavern painted salmon pink, which squats in the middle of the village like a hideous strawberry blancmange: The Rose and Castle Inn, according to faded letters painted directly on the wall. My nerves increase. The coachman takes us on up the road, towards a squat brick church on the right and a collection of ramshackle redbrick buildings behind a low brick wall on the left. Beyond them rises a low hillock set back from the road, crowned by a heap of grey boulders which are scattered about with no apparent design. Our carriage draws to a halt. 'There you are,' says our driver, who has jumped down to fit some steps to the back of the wagonette. 'The castle. Do you want to walk about, or what?'

We contemplate the strewn rocks. 'There must be some mistake,' I say. 'Isn't there another castle in Dalkenny? A proper one?'

'I'm sorry it's not good enough for yer ladyship,' he mutters in a surly fashion, adding something to the effect the ruin's over a thousand years old so what did we expect: curtains and a mat at the door?

One part of my fuddled brain is still thinking, 'But how can Mr Hamilton-Greene have inherited an ancient monument?'

'Never mind,' says Mrs Johnson, climbing nimbly down the steps and peering back the way we've come. 'Let's have a look round that darling little church.' Shooting me a look that's half-concerned, half-reproachful, Julia follows her down the road.

I stand for a moment, rooted by indecision and a dawning sense that things are not as they should be, before walking up the slope to examine the ruins and decide what to do next. The stones offer no clue. I feel the coachman's malevolent stare on the back of my neck so, after a short saunter about, I turn around and make towards the church myself. On the way, however, I happen to notice a sign fixed to the wall enclosing the red-brick settlement. 'Castlemount,' it reads.

The name is suddenly horribly familiar. I stare at the place: a loose collection of outbuildings arranged around a yard with a fairly substantial house to one side. And as I stand looking over the wall, Mr Hamilton-Greene emerges from one of those buildings, his hands in his pockets. Whistling. Oh, but he's more handsome than ever – in breeches, a rough cambric shirt and billycock hat with a red spotted scarf knotted carelessly at his throat. My heart turns over. Pushing open a gate, I enter the premises without further ado and start to cross the yard towards him. He looks up as I approach. Even in my current state of delusion, I notice the look of horror that comes over his face.

I cannot recast this encounter with the benefit of hindsight, much as I'd like to, so here is an exact record of our conversation: each word being seared by shame upon my memory.

'Oh, Mr Hamilton-Greene,' I cry. 'Don't worry! I have only come to support you.'

He stares at me blankly, and then he says, 'Holy Mary, Mother of God. How in the name of creation

Eugenie's Story

did you find me?' His brogue, I happen to notice, seems more pronounced on his native soil.

'That doesn't matter,' I say breathlessly. 'All that counts is now I am here, and we can settle this unfortunate misunderstanding.'

'Have you come on your own?' he asks, looking about in a shifty manner.

'I'm with my friends the Johnsons,' I tell him. 'They're currently exploring the church.'

'Well, that won't take long,' he says. 'Will they be coming to find you after that?'

The light rain that has been drizzling all morning is beginning to fall more steadily. 'Shall we go into the house?' I suggest. It feels inappropriate to be talking about important matters in a stableyard.

He seems reluctant, however, and I can hardly insist, so we carry on standing there awkwardly. 'Look, I'm sorry things turned out the way they did,' he says. 'If that's what you've come all this way to hear.'

'But how *did* they turn out?' I ask. 'I have no idea. You must know there is talk of impropriety. Will you return to London and explain what has happened? Perhaps your cousin could come too. Is he here at the moment?' I glance again towards the house.

'He's gone away,' says Mr HG. 'To America. Turns out the horse wasn't such a great beast after all, that's the thing.'

'But it might improve,' I say, 'with time, and proper training. Perhaps we could go and see it together?'

'No,' he says, 'it's dead. It broke its leg, so it did, and had to be shot. Terrible bad luck.'

'Well then, come back with me and tell that to my brother,' I say, starting towards him.

He recoils. 'I can't. I must stay here for the time being. I'm sorry but there it is, nothing to be done. Well, goodbye, Miss Vye.' He begins to back away. 'Grand to see you and all that.'

I can't believe it. 'But you said you'd come back for me!' I say, my voice rising with emotion. 'You said we'd go riding together again in the moonlight!'

It's unbearable to see him so evasive, his beautiful mouth saying such ordinary things, and the gulf between us that can never be bridged. My dream is vanishing and the harder I try to cling on to it, the faster it slips through my fingers.

'Can I help you?' I turn to see a middle-aged lady in a tweed costume staring at me suspiciously. She has a shelf-like bosom and grey hair drawn into a straggly bun. The hem of her skirt is splashed with mud and a piece of straw protrudes from her sleeve. Drawing myself up, I attempt to regain some shred of dignity and say the first thing that comes into my head: that I am visiting friends in the area and have just dropped by.

'Then let me offer you some refreshment,' she

says. 'Come into the house for a moment, young lady.'

Mr Hamilton-Greene is already retreating towards the barn from which he emerged. The rain is tippling down and I am defeated; I hardly care what happens. I follow my companion into the house, wondering vaguely who she might be. Mr Hamilton-Greene's mother, perhaps? When we are sitting in a shabby drawing room she introduces herself; I instantly forget her name but it's not Hamilton-Greene. I tell her mine is Elizabeth Cheesman, and that I can't stay long because friends are expecting me back shortly.

We sit for a while in silence, and then she says, narrowing her eyes at me, 'It's green, isn't it?'

I look down at my blouse, which is blue. 'In certain lights, perhaps,' I begin, thinking that nothing anyone says could surprise me now, or indeed affect me in any way at all. 'But maybe turquoise would be nearer the mark.'

'Oh, don't play the innocent with me,' she snaps. 'I know perfectly well what you're up to. I'm talking about Patrick Green. You're trying to take him away from me, aren't you? Sidling up to him in the yard and promising all sorts of inducements, no doubt. Well, you're not the first and you probably won't be the last. But I can tell you now, you won't succeed.'

I shift in my chair, horror-stricken, stammering

something to the effect she must be mistaken and anyway I have no idea what she means. It's all too dreadful for words. What is this ghastly woman implying?

'You can offer him more money but he won't take it,' she says. 'He's like a son to me. I gave him all my late husband's clothes and Nigel was the best-dressed man in County Meath. Besides, he's just had three weeks off in London for his cousin's funeral – that's where you came across him, I suppose. Well, you can take yourself back there to find a groom. You're not having mine.'

Uttering an inarticulate cry, pressing a trembling hand to my mouth, I stand up. 'Yes,' says the horrid coarse creature with grim satisfaction, 'I thought that was your little game. As if dressing yourself up like a dog's dinner would make any difference.'

I run from the room, almost knocking over the maid who is approaching with a tea tray. Blindly I fumble at the front door before at last gaining my freedom and rushing away down the road, hardly caring who might be watching.

I have opened my heart to a servant. A groom has kissed me.

I cannot endure the shame.

*

I remember very little of our departure from Dalkenny or the journey back to Dublin. Confused pictures float through my mind: leaning against a gravestone in the churchyard while Julia asked me in a low voice whatever was the matter; the coachman's expression as I was helped sobbing into the wagonette; the line of small children sitting on a wall who watched us leave, mouths agape in their grubby round faces like so many seed potatoes. I caught the Johnsons exchanging anxious glances but couldn't bring myself to explain my distress – not even when Julia came to my hotel room that night to ask what on earth had happened. All I could do was shake my head, tears still coursing down my cheeks. Thank heavens Julia didn't say 'I told you so,' but then again, she didn't need to. She left me alone to wallow in my misery, and her silent disapproval was more eloquent than words could ever have been.

I stayed in my room for most of the next day, and the day after that, while the Johnsons explored Dublin. It was as much as I could do to let Beth dress me each morning and then, when everyone else had left, totter out to a bench on St Stephen's Green where I sat alone in abject misery. I hardly ate or slept. As soon as I closed my eyes, visions of that man's face appeared before me and I heard again certain phrases of his – or worse still, mine – which startled me awake, groaning with humiliation and despair. How could I have been so utterly mistaken? What if my conduct became common knowledge? I'd never be able to hold my head up in society again. Then anger would take the place of shame. I had been most shabbily treated through no fault of my own; except that of being too open and trusting. The only useful thing I managed to do was write to Plum, stating that in fact we had bumped into Mr Hamilton-Greene – or Patrick Green as he should perhaps more properly be called – and my confidence in the man had been sadly misplaced. He was a groom at Castlemount, Dalkenny, in County Meath, and little more than a common thief. (I asked him to keep my involvement in this discovery a strict secret, of course.)

*

After three sleepless nights, the time came for our return to London. That morning Beth helped me into the clothes she had chosen. I hardly cared what they were. As we left the streets of Dublin behind, I couldn't help remembering the foolish state of anticipation in which I'd arrived at the city. The thought of resuming the life I'd left with such high hopes seemed impossible; I no longer had the heart for balls and dinner parties. Kingstown Harbour was busy with cattle ships taking livestock over to England. I gazed upon the piteous faces and wild rolling eyes of those poor beasts, deeming myself in a similar situation but to be denied the blessed relief of an abattoir on arrival. The idea of casting myself overboard mid-journey seemed the only solution to my predicament. All I had to decide was the most opportune spot and moment.

Two hours into our journey, therefore, when Julia had retreated ashen-faced to the ladies' room and Mrs Johnson was taking refreshment in the saloon, I climbed upstairs and walked about on deck as if innocently taking the air. A huddle of third-class passengers sat on the starboard side of the steamer beneath tarpaulins and umbrellas. Beth was not among them. She'd made such a fuss about having to sit on deck for the previous journey that Mrs Johnson had paid for a seat below the hatches where she was presently languishing: about as much use to anyone as a yard of pump water. I made my way to the stern of the ship and stared down into the swirling depths. A wide path of foam streamed out behind us, so clean and white against the dark blue water. I imagined sinking down into it, absolved of my sins and finally at peace, and gripped the rail more tightly prior to climbing over. Unfortunately at that moment a sudden gust of wind sneaked under the brim of my bonnet – the navy straw with a crown of pink roses – and tore it off my head amid a shower of hatpins. With an involuntary cry of dismay, I watched my poor hat cartwheel bravely over the wake until, finally conquered by the churning waves, it sank to a watery grave. One pink satin rose bobbed up to the surface and floated there for a moment, before it too was swallowed up for good.

I couldn't help but picture myself in the sea, skirts and petticoats billowing about me, hair swirling around my shoulders like seaweed. How long would *I* take to disappear from view? What if I were spotted, and somebody threw me a life preserver, or risked their own life trying to save me? Being rescued would be the worst of all worlds: I should have to pretend I'd fallen in by mistake and would end up looking even more of a fool. Perhaps I should load my pockets with rocks to speed up the process, although I couldn't imagine where rocks were to be found on a mail steamer. Heavy parcels might have to do instead. That would be unfair on their intended recipients, however, and how could I climb over the rail with packages concealed about my person? People might think I was trying to steal them.

As I was contemplating these and similar questions, I felt a hand grip my elbow and looked round to see Mrs Johnson standing beside me, determination and disapproval written in equal measures over her small plain face. 'I think you owe me an apology,' she said, 'or at least an explanation.'

I allowed myself to be led down to the saloon, where we sat in a quiet corner away from the crowd. Mrs Johnson poured me a tot of brandy from her hipflask and said she gathered from Julia there was some ulterior motive behind our expedition, to which she had not been privy. She explained the difficulty in which I had placed both her and Julia, and the fact that if anything improper had occurred (which I assured her was not the case) she would have been blamed for leading me to my ruin, no matter how innocently. 'After all the hospitality your family has shown us! Can you imagine how angry Kate and your parents would have been with me? And rightly so.'

Despite my initial shock at being spoken to in such a forthright manner, I listened to what she had to say. Well, I had to; there was no escape. It was painful to admit that yes, I had been selfish, thinking only of myself and ignoring the effect my actions would have on others. 'I don't know all the details of this escapade,' Mrs Johnson continued, 'and actually, I'm not sure I want to. As far as I'm concerned the matter is over, but I hope you will learn a lesson from it.'

She gave me another tot of brandy – which I've discovered is a most efficacious cure for *mal de mer* – and left me alone to ponder her advice. Laying my (hatless) head against the pitching, tossing banquette, I sank into exhausted sleep.

*

We arrived back in Eaton Square to find Mama and Aunt Georgina there alone (Papa having gone to Swallowcliffe, Kate to the Dower House and Edward staying at his club). After changing out of my travel-soiled clothes, I hurried to Julia's room. I found her lying down with a flannel soaked in eau-de-cologne over her forehead but she was prepared to listen to me as I knelt beside the bed. It cost me dearly to do so, but I admitted she had been right and I had been wrong. Our trip to Ireland had been ill-advised and I would be most grateful if it was never referred to it again, or mentioned to anyone else. With a wave of her hand, she indicated her agreement, and wordlessly we embraced.

Last night I managed to fall asleep a little more easily and only woke twice in the small hours, groaning and muttering. This morning I attended both the early- and mid-morning services at St Peter's Church, and spent the afternoon playing Chopin *études* on the piano and reading *Paradise Lost* in our silent drawing-room, accompanied only by the ticking of the clock. (*Sonnets from the Portuguese*, my first choice, were simply too poignant.) Part of my spirit has been torn away and trampled underfoot. I am no more substantial than a puff of thistledown, drifting hither and thither at the whim of any passing breeze. Oh, how sharply the dagger of remorse pierces my heart! How heavy the load I must bear!

Julia and Mrs Johnson went out and about this afternoon, returning with two pieces of news. Firstly, the Duchess of Clarebourne has passed away in Italy, which is a great shock as we had no idea she was so ill. I shall write to dear Plum with my condolences: from one suffering soul to another, though of course he doesn't know the extent of my predicament. Secondly, they bumped into Lord McGillie and the Duxfords by the Achilles statue, and His Lordship was most interested to hear we had come back from Ireland. He intends to call tomorrow morning; no doubt expecting my answer to his proposal. I haven't the first idea what to say. I don't love him – but what does that matter? Look where love brought me. I should like some time to consider the offer but time is another luxury I don't have. Apparently Miss Pratt arrived at the house yesterday to present an envelope from Madame Angeline, addressed to me, which is currently lying unopened on top of the bureau. I know only too well what it contains.

I hardly care what is to become of my life. Monkton Abbey, Duxford Hall, a hill station in India: they're all one and the same. Like Adam and Eve in *Paradise Lost*, I must make my way through the world 'with wandering steps and slow.' Shall I ever find a place to rest, or a hand to hold on this wearisome journey?

Wednesday April 26th
I'd decided to let Lord McGillie speak first this morning before formulating my response, which was just as well in the circumstances. He started talking in his own inimitable fashion to reveal that, on reflection, he felt his earlier conversation with me had been too hasty. In our absence he'd realized the person best suited to be his bride was Charlotte Duxford, and he hoped I would have the kindness to release him from his initial proposal to me, which had been made 'in the heat of the moment'. (I forbore from pointing out he had seemed fairly temperate at the time.)

So fate has played its part and I am *not* now to become Lady McGillie. I found myself utterly indifferent to the news and was able to reply that in fact I'd come to exactly the same conclusion myself and was about to tell him so. (Not about Charlotte's eligibility, of course: a matter upon which I can't possibly presume to comment.) 'Jolly good! Jolly good!' he kept repeating with an evident sense of relief, and started to sidle out of the room. However it now occurred to me that I was letting him off far too lightly, and anger took the place of resignation. He had raised the matter of marriage in the first place and dropped it just as capriciously, without any thought to my feelings. And he'd come to our house empty-handed: not even so much as a bunch of flowers or small item of jewellery by way of apology.

Although I wasn't at all upset, I had every reason to be.

'Just a minute,' I commanded, and the consequent look of fear crossing his shifty face only increased my irritation. I had no idea how to continue – until suddenly the account from Madame Angeline seemed to leap before my eyes. 'Before I realized our betrothal would be a terrible mistake,' I went on, 'I'd ordered some new clothes for my position as your fiancée, and the dressmaker has already started work. Naturally, I assumed…' Delicacy prevented me from continuing the sentence; I merely fetched the envelope and held it out to him with steely resolve.

'Oh, of course,' he said, pocketing it with alacrity. 'Quite understand. Don't say another word.'

'She's also designing me an evening gown,' I continued. 'Shall I ask for the account to be sent to you?'

He bridled at this but I didn't care; I'd remembered that Millicent Shoosmith had received an undisclosed sum of money from a guardsman who'd let her down. He'd proposed in writing and given her a ring, and she'd had to threaten to take him to court – but still, Lord M was getting off lightly with only a dressmaker's bill to settle and he knew it.

'Another evening gown, you say?' he repeated, playing for time. 'Just the one more, I assume.'

Graciously I inclined my head and we shook

hands as though concluding a business arrangement, which I suppose is exactly what it was. Odious little man: Charlotte's welcome to him.

Friday April 28th

Mama has decided she will chaperone me herself from now on and sent Aunt Georgina off to the Isle of Wight. The news of Lord McGillie's engagement to Charlotte Duxford seems to have filled her with strengthened resolve as far as my prospects are concerned: one last hurrah, perhaps. The thought of her critical eyes watching my every move might once have filled me with dread, but now I can hardly find the energy to care. What does it matter where I go or whom I meet? It is all meaningless.

I fear news of my second failed engagement may have spread abroad. When collecting a pair of new riding boots at Peal and Bartley's yesterday, we ran into Millicent Shoosmith, who said she was surprised not to have seen me at the Galbraiths' on Tuesday evening; had I been unwell? She must have known I hadn't been sent an invitation. Still, I've always suspected the Galbraiths were fair-weather friends, and Julia was there to squeeze my hand in silent sympathy.

I can't bear to contemplate the Johnsons' planned return to America in September. Perhaps I might ask to go back with them for a visit instead of being dispatched to India? In the meantime, I am lifting my gaze from this cruel world to a better one.

Eugenie's Story

I've been spending so long in St Peter's the curate is beginning to look alarmed and flees to the sacristy whenever I appear. I read improving texts rather than novels or the *Strand Magazine*, denying myself even the comfort of Raffles and Sherlock Holmes, and only go to balls and sales in aid of charitable causes. Since I no longer walk about by the Achilles statue at mid-day, I miss invitations to the delightfully casual luncheon parties I used to enjoy; I have no stomach for them now. I cannot bring myself to look anyone in the face, fearing they might somehow be able to read the extent of my shame in my eyes.

My one frivolity has been a trip to Madame Angeline's with Julia, to collect her gowns which are now ready and to order my own: the Tarbert model, as I call it privately. Mrs Thompson was all sweetness and light so I assume His Lordship has settled my account. I instructed her not to stint on the detail and she's surpassed herself: ivory satin lined with pink to create a subtle blush-rose effect, the corsage, *jupe* and train trimmed with trails of silk roses and knots of pale-pink satin ribbon. I feel none of the innocent pleasure a new frock used to induce, however: merely a cold sense of satisfaction that Lord McGillie, at least, has had to pay for trifling with my affections. Charlotte and her mother have already called to receive our congratulations, which I've most fulsomely bestowed; Mama rather less so. I bear Charlotte no ill will. *Au contraire*, I am grateful to her for rescuing me from a dreadful *mésalliance*.

I cannot bring myself to think about that disastrous episode in Ireland, although the memory of it hangs like a dark cloud constantly over my head. I make an effort to smile for Julia's sake because I know she's worried about me, but melancholy has my heart in a vice-like grip. Now I must watch other girls surrounded by their beaux, wanting only solitude in which to nurse my wounded spirits.

Wednesday May 10th

Scarcely the energy to write my journal. The days blur into each another. The season has opened with the usual private view at the Royal Academy, and Mary Galbraith is engaged to William Gifford; I hardly care. Even the Guards' theatricals at Chelsea Barracks bring no more than a faint smile to my lips. Henry Duxford, who has arranged our seats, asks anxiously whether I'm feeling ill. Mama draws me to one side to say she approves of this new serious demeanour but perhaps I'm taking things a little far. Typically she assumes any emotion is only pretence.

Princess May attends the theatricals, radiant in white silk and pearls, the Duke of York on one side and her father on the other. Lucky, lucky Princess May, with her pure and simple heart, and so much to look forward to! And yet she has also known tragedy, having lost her first fiancé, the Duke's older brother, to pneumonia six weeks after their engagement. We have a great deal in common – although to be perfectly honest, I cannot imagine her ever having loved Prince Albert as I loved Freddie. Albert Victor always looked such a cold fish, and he'd been engaged twice before. Mama said at the time it was a blessing in disguise.

Friday May 12th

Today I met Plum in St Peter's, quite by chance. He was alone in a pew at the back of the church, looking so lonely I had to go and sit with him. The curate and a lady arranging flowers were there too, so it seemed perfectly respectable for us to be talking privately together. Anyway the Duke, like Caesar's wife, is beyond reproach.

'Thank you for sending word from Ireland,' he said. 'I only hope you didn't have too distressing a time over there. I feel perfectly wretched about the whole affair, to be honest. What on earth possessed me to bring such a fellow to Swallowcliffe? Your stepmother still isn't talking to me.'

But really, one can't blame the Duke for being deceived along with the rest of us. He told me Edward had passed Mr Hamilton-Greene's address to the police but apparently when enquiries were made, the wretch was found to have left the village. So Mrs Castlemount, whatever her name is, has lost her groom anyway; I find myself rather glad to hear that. 'One lives and learns,' I said, suddenly exhausted by the very memory.

It was comforting sitting there in the cool

shadowy church. 'Perhaps I should become a nun,' I mused aloud. 'Don't you think that would be a restful sort of way to live? In a retreat somewhere, with only birdsong and chanting to disturb one's quiet contemplation.'

Plum didn't think my motivation was sufficiently spiritual, however, and wondered whether I was in fact suited to the religious life. 'You are so young,' he added kindly, patting my knee. 'There'll be plenty of time for quiet contemplation later.'

I offered my condolences again on the passing of his wife, which he graciously accepted. We have both lost our taste for society but knew we should probably meet at some function or another: Araminta's wedding, if not before. The Duke isn't so very old, I thought as we parted, and still a handsome man; he has the chance to find happiness with somebody else. For now though, he and I need a little peace to lick our wounds.

Monday May 15th

This afternoon Mama and I attended a drawing-room meeting at the house of Mrs Ernest Franklin to discuss the Girls' Games Club, which has just been founded with the aim of giving London girls the chance to play cricket, hockey and other such sporting activities. They have taken a small patch of ground near Wormwood Scrubs and engaged two teachers. I was wondering about offering to assist there but have settled for sewing tabards instead – or rather, instructing Beth to sew them. I am going to devote more time to good causes and this seems an appropriate place to start.

As we were leaving Mrs Franklin's house we bumped into a fair-haired young man whom she introduced as her nephew; he gave me a most unsettling stare. Quite inappropriate for the occasion, and I rebuffed him as openly as politeness allowed.

Thursday May 18th

To the *soirée* of the Society of Lady Artists. A great crush and the rooms so hot, I felt faint. Mrs Marrable received in a gown of grey brocade trimmed with red velvet. Caught a glimpse of the fair-haired young man goggling at me and frowned again most severely in his direction. However he placed a chair for me by an open window, which was at least useful. His name is Captain Jonathan Hughes-Hampton.

Saturday May 20th

It seems I am destined never to escape the attentions of Captain Hughes-Hampton. For one thing, I have discovered his mother is a friend of Mama's. She (Mama that is, not Lady HH) is clearly delighted he seems struck with me and keeps looking at me sideways, as if unable to believe my good fortune. Then yesterday we attended a polo match at the Hurlingham Club in which Rory was playing, and there was the Captain again – charging about all over the field and letting fly with his mallet to great effect.

Polo is the most exciting sport to watch, so fast and furious, but surely better suited to warriors on the Persian plains than the sedate surroundings of Hurlingham: all cucumber sandwiches, Battenberg cake and the clink of teaspoons in bone-china saucers. It turns out Captain Hughes-Hampton is a member of the Life Guards so he knows Rory in the Blues, but not as intimately as one would a fellow-officer. He was riding a wiry black pony, quick and supple as a snake, and one couldn't help but admire his sporting prowess. However I was not in much of a mood to make myself agreeable, as once I would have done, and let Julia and her mother pay the necessary compliments when the Captain came over to talk to us. I merely remarked when the occasion arose that he and his horse seemed perfectly suited. 'Snappiest little thing I ever sat on,' he declared. 'Not the prettiest pony on the field but she can run rings round them all. Ride too, do you?'

When I admitted I did, he said I should have a turn on the mare whenever I wanted. Riding is my main solace at the moment but I prefer going out before breakfast in Hyde Park when no one else is about, with only a groom for company. 'On some old nag from the livery stables? Can't have that,' he said, pressing various horses upon me. I politely refused, not wanting to be beholden to anybody, but he wouldn't take no for an answer and persisted until I had finally agreed to take out another mare of his, stabled at the barracks in Hyde Park. Well, at least I know he is *bona fide*, unlike a certain other gentleman with a double-barrelled name.

Mama hasn't mentioned hydrotherapy or India for a while, thank goodness. Connie writes to say the monsoon rains have come and her shoes are covered with mildew.

Tuesday May 30th

I am now officially admitted to have an admirer. Of course it is all very proper and I only ever meet Captain HH in the company of at least Mama and usually several others besides. He cannot accept I'm in no mood for mingling with the fashionable crowd, but the strange thing is, turning down his advances only seems to make him doubly determined. 'Men never care for anything they are sure of,' Mama once told me; I should have paid her more attention. So far he has invited me to Ascot and Wimbledon, a picnic at Kew Gardens, luncheon with his mother and sisters at Kettner's, and performances at both the opera and the theatre. I've made various excuses but it seems the more determined I am to withdraw from society, the harder he tries to pull me in.

He's exactly the sort of man I ought to marry: well-bred, ambitious, striking rather than handsome, with blond hair that glistens like corn stubble, a pale complexion and light blue eyes. His grandfather was a Danish sea captain and there's definitely something of the marauding Viking about his looks. I'm afraid

Julia doesn't like him; she's never said so directly but I can tell from her expression whenever his name is mentioned. Still, she can't be expected to understand an Englishman of the traditional type – which is exactly Kate's problem, now I come to think of it. From what Julia's told me, American girls enjoy a greater degree of freedom than their English sisters, both in thought and action, and I suppose they're not used to being restrained in any way. Of course I wish Julia could be happy for me, but she will be going back to America in a few months' time and I must make plans for a life without her support – painful though that is to contemplate. What I should dearly like is for her to marry an Englishman and stay here, but so far she doesn't seem to have any particular favourites.

The fear of running into Araminta unexpectedly has lessened, because several people have seen the Captain paying me attention and it's not inconceivable he might at some stage have proposed to me, or be about to. And slowly, little by little, I am beginning to recover from the humiliation of Ireland. If the Captain notices a certain emptiness where my heart should be, it doesn't trouble him, and perhaps this remoteness even adds to my allure. He must never know of my shame; far better he should think me cold than ridiculous.

Tuesday June 13th
Life goes on. Having received word from Madame

Eugenie's Story

Angeline the Tarbert gown was ready, last Friday I went to collect it with Julia and Beth. It occurred to me in the hansom on the way there that we might bump into Charlotte Duxford and her mother, ordering a wedding gown or trousseau. I refuse to feel guilty about my arrangement with Lord McGillie in front of Charlotte – after all, if she were a different sort of girl and slightly more prepossessing, one might accuse her of stealing him away from me – but it might have been awkward. Still, no doubt Mrs Thompson would have carried off the situation with her usual aplomb. Looking around at the various beauties intent on beautifying themselves still further, I wondered how many of them were having accounts settled by gentlemen who would prefer to remain anonymous. (Julia knows nothing of His Lordship's involvement in my affairs, incidentally, of which I'm sure she and her mother would disapprove.)

    I feel like a different girl from the one who met Araminta in that gracious room not so very long ago: about twenty years older, for one thing, and much more worldly-wise. 'You see?' Mrs Thompson observed during the fitting. 'I predicted your success and so it has come to pass. A little bird tells me you have captured the heart of a certain cavalry officer, Miss Vye, as well as yon Scottish lord.' She did not endear herself to me with this remark, which I thought indiscreet, and a rather silly way of talking besides. I merely observed that gossip travelled quickly but could not always be trusted.

The following evening Mama had arranged a supper party for the Hughes-Hamptons, so my gown was ready just in time. The fact Papa had travelled up from Swallowcliffe to be with us made the occasion seem especially significant, and I had to confess to the faintest flutter of nerves when dressing – only compounded when Mama sent Agnes along the landing with her diamonds for me to wear. It was perfectly obvious Lord HH and his wife wanted to look me over as a potential daughter-in-law. A few months ago I would have been in a terrible state but now the strongest emotion I can manage is mild anxiety. Nothing seems to matter much any more – although unfortunately my hands are still troublesome, when one might have expected an improvement in their condition as a result of my catatonia. Thank goodness for kid gloves.

The gown certainly looked delightful and Beth had persuaded me to wear the Botticelli wreath, so I was confident of my appearance. Lord HH was pleasant enough: rather high colour in his cheeks and plagued by gout, but most appreciative of the food and Papa's choice of claret. With the Johnsons, Rory, Kate and Edward, and an elderly neighbour to make up the numbers (taking the place of the Duke of Clarebourne, with whom Mama is still cross for having brought a certain person to our house, but whose charm and wit were much missed), we made twelve at the table. I sat opposite Mrs Johnson, who kept looking at me in an appraising manner, or so it seemed; I'm not sure she has completely forgiven me. It was a splendid meal – two soups (one hot, one cold), Dover sole and trout, roast lamb and quails with numerous vegetables – finished off by a chocolate bombe and our own peaches and grapes, sent up in the weekly hamper from Swallowcliffe. Lady HH spoke to Papa and Edward about gardening and the servant problem; Lord HH and Mama discussed the perils, both social and financial, of entertaining the Prince of Wales; Julia and Mrs Johnson described the coast of New England in some detail to Rory; the elderly neighbour, a retired archaeologist, lectured Kate about a Roman city somewhere that is in the process of being excavated. The Captain and I talked almost exclusively about hunting. His family home is an Elizabethan manor house in Leicestershire and he rides with the Quorn, who are about to elect a new Master, so we managed to keep the conversation going with a discussion about possible candidates.

There was an indefinable rightness about the evening, I observed, looking round the candle-lit table. Nobody had raised controversial matters such as Irish Home Rule or unsuccessful business partnerships; the conversation was designed purely to establish mutual interests and friendship rather than to snipe or provoke. Relations between Kate and Edward weren't particularly warm but they managed to present a united front, as did my father and stepmother, and no one would have guessed the recent tensions between them. Lord HH had been at school with Papa; he referred to my father as 'Viney' while Papa called him 'Bunt', for reasons best known to themselves. I'm sure they had many reminiscences to exchange over port and cigars.

We ladies retired to the drawing room at Mama's signal, there indulging in a lively discussion about the conduct of certain Professional Beauties, and whether one ought to acknowledge an actress in public. Lady HH had met Lily Langtry at Plum's and, coming across her walking down Piccadilly the next morning, hadn't known whether to avert her eyes. (She'd compromised by crossing the road.) She then hinted the poor Duke had been landed with his late wife's gambling debts, but Mama changed the subject swiftly and it was not referred to again.

Only the Johnsons seemed a little out of place. When Mrs Johnson was introduced to Lady HH at the beginning of the evening, Her Ladyship declared in tones of wonder that she'd never met an American before, and I detected a certain *froideur* in Mrs Johnson's response. And it's not Julia's fault but of course she doesn't know many of the people of whom we spoke, so couldn't contribute much of interest. I could see Lady HH dismissing her as dull.

Eugenie's Story

On my own account, however, I knew from the way Mama bade me goodnight that I'd passed muster. It strikes me as ironic that the less effort I make in social situations, the more success I seem to have.

*

Julia was tired and went straight to bed so we did not discuss the evening in our usual fashion, and I didn't like to mention the subject at breakfast the next morning in front of Mama. I'd had a visit to the British Museum in mind for a while as a suitably improving activity, so after church, I asked Julia whether she would like to accompany me there that afternoon. As we wandered round the echoing (and frankly, somewhat depressing) Elgin Saloon, contemplating the ruined marbles, I tried to explain about Captain Hughes-Hampton: about his suitability, our mutual expectations and the likelihood of their being satisfied. 'But why choose him in particular?' Julia said when I'd finished speaking. 'What is it about him that appeals to you? I only ask because you don't seem particularly animated in his company.'

'I'm no longer the foolish creature I was,' I replied. 'I have shed any wild delusions of love and submitted to the way of the world.'

'But at least then you were alive!' she exclaimed, her eyes gleaming. (She does have remarkably pretty eyes, although on the small side.) 'You might have been foolish but there was some spark about you. I'd sooner have the old Eugenie, even if she was as mad as a March hare, than this ladylike automaton. I'm sorry but I can't pretend to like your captain, or his mother, and I don't think you really like him either. Not deep down. He's so...brutal. Did you see the way he whipped his horse? And the way he reacts to anyone who disagrees with him? You don't have to marry him just because your stepmother approves and your fathers were at school together.'

'I could do a lot worse,' I snapped, for now she'd succeeded in nettling 'And you could do a lot better. What about Henry Duxford, who's so kind and charming, and obviously mad about you?'

'Henry Duxford has been mad about me for years,' I said. 'But he's a perfectly pleasant nonentity, and I refuse to be commonplace.'

She threw up her hands at this and marched away. We spent some time separately gazing at headless, armless and footless Greeks in various attitudes of despair until I had simmered down and crossed the room to apologize – something at which I'm becoming quite adept these days.

My apology was accepted, but with a condition attached. 'Could you bring yourself to tell me something of what happened in Ireland?' Julia asked. 'I know you don't want to talk about it but you've been so subdued ever since.'

'I lost my innocence there,' I said – adding hastily on seeing her expression of alarm, 'Not literally, of course. I bared my soul, only to find my most cherished dreams trampled upon, my every assumption proved false, my confidence shattered. I need somebody strong like Captain Hughes-Hampton to control my worst excesses.'

'Oh, Genie,' she sighed. 'Just because you've made one mistake, it doesn't mean you have to make another. Please don't rush into this decision. Mother and I have decided to visit Paris, to see the Impressionist paintings and take in a little shopping. Will you come with us? Some time abroad would do you the world of good, I'm sure. At least it will give you a chance to think things over.'

'But look what happened the last time we three went away together,' I said. 'Do you think your mother will risk another excursion?'

Julia thought she would as long as I promised to behave and said that anyway, Kate was coming too so we would be four not three, and she was also considering inviting the Duxfords, as Henry was particularly interesting and well-informed about art, 'for a nonentity' (I can see that's a remark I shan't live down in a hurry), and Charlotte would probably like to order her wedding gown.

I pointed out that Paris would soon be deserted as the fashionable set leave town much earlier there, but she said that was part of the appeal; she and her mother were finding the London season a little strenuous, and the prospect of wandering round such a beautiful place in peace was most attractive. After a moment's contemplation, I found it so too. I feel at home in France: *bons mots* trip naturally off my tongue, I adore the food, and French women have such indefinable chic. As a matter of fact I have been mistaken for a native on both my previous visits to the country. It would also be helpful for the Johnsons to have somebody in their party who can speak French; Julia has apparently learned the language but I can't imagine her accent is up to much. So I told her I would be delighted to be included in their plans, and was very pleased to have been asked. Whereupon we embraced, agreed we couldn't bear to hide anything from each other, and strolled away from the dreary antiquities, arm-in-arm. 'I only have your best interests at heart,' Julia said, and I knew that was true.

A few days away will give me the chance to clear my head and view the Captain from afar before I pledge myself to him for ever. My one reservation is that I might return to find him enamoured of somebody else, as was the case with Lord McGillie, but given his character and our history so far, I think a short absence will only make his heart grow fonder.

Mama seems to agree. She remarks I am becoming 'quite the strategist' and has given me permission to go to Paris. The Johnsons, Kate and I are to leave at the end of the week, after Araminta's wedding: an event which I am privately dreading.

Eugenie's Story

Mama says she does not mind being left alone in London again and will try to amuse herself somehow.

The newspapers are full of details about the forthcoming wedding of Princess May and the Duke of York, which is to take place in July. The Duke has given his bride-to-be a necklace comprising five rows of pearls with a diamond clasp in the form of a rose; the Duchess of Teck has presented her daughter with a tiara of diamonds and turquoise, and she has received further jewels, plate and china too numerous to mention, including a fan of white ostrich feathers mounted in ivory and gold set with diamonds from the South African community in England. I am very happy for her.

Friday June 16th

So, Araminta's wedding yesterday. It is held at midday and since Hanover Square is only a short distance from our temporary home in Bedford Square, Mama and I go there on foot. Papa has already returned to Swallowcliffe, pleading urgent estate business. Mama looks elegant in pearls and a gown of cream brocade and I am carefully understated in pale-blue satin with a ravishing picture hat; a certain amount of trouble has been taken, I hope to convey, but not too much. Weddings are bittersweet occasions for a person in my position and this one above all others is bound to evoke painful memories. As the poet says, 'Joy and woe are woven fine, clothing for the soul divine.' Yet I am determined to be happy for Araminta, and sincerely wish her every blessing as the future Mrs Fishburne from the bottom of my heart. We have presented the happy couple with a china umbrella stand which has already been delivered to the house.

Mr Fishburne's people look presentable but less distinguished than the FitzWilliams' friends and family, and I feel we are definitely sitting on the right side of the church (although it is in fact the left side, literally speaking, as we are guests of the bride). Several people acknowledge us and shortly before the service is due to begin, I see Plum make a discreet entrance in a black frock coat. My heart goes out to him. I remember only too well how it feels to cast a shadow by virtue of one's very presence in mourning: a visible reminder of the fate that awaits us all. And then a slender figure appears in the sunlit church doorway, her silhouette outlined in fiery light: Araminta, on her father's arm, swathed in white mousseline de soie and the priceless FitzWilliam lace I had once envisaged wearing. I cannot help but shed a surreptitious tear. Mama has no need to look so disapproving: handkerchiefs are blossoming like flowers all over the church. There is something unbearably poignant about the hopeful, tremulous figure walking slowly down the aisle towards her chosen prince. Lawrence Fishburne is tall and gangly, and I happen to notice he has enormous feet, but he's gazing at Araminta with a look of adoration that transforms his undistinguished features.

A charming service, we all agree afterwards, crossing Hanover Square to Brixham House for the wedding breakfast; the flowers are splendid and the bride is both beautiful and happy. 'A love match,' sighs an elderly matron, dolefully shaking her head. I search for Plum, whom as usual these days Mama has ignored, only to see him slipping away alone. It seems dreadful he should have to leave like a thief in the night without a friendly word from anyone, so I hurry after him. He appears pleased to see me. We take a turn round the gardens in the middle of the square and sit by the statue of William Pitt the Younger, whose grave face watches us impassively. We are both in philosophical mood once more. Just as I am thinking of Freddie and the life we might have shared together, I suppose Plum is remembering his own wedding and mourning his wife, despite her shortcomings.

'What do you think is the secret of a happy marriage?' I ask him, as a vision of the Captain and myself standing at the altar comes into my head – realizing too late, alas, this is probably a tactless question.

'Try to find someone you like,' he says. 'Someone with similar interests, whose company you enjoy. The rest is all flim-flam.'

He makes it sound so easy. We say our goodbyes before my absence from the party can be noted; just before we part, I tell the Duke about our proposed trip to Paris. He says he may well see us there, owing to the small matter of a château in his possession that needs to be sold. So perhaps Lady Hughes-Hampton was right about the Duchess's debts, although it was most indiscreet of her to have mentioned the subject.

I return to the wedding breakfast, which passes without incident and moderately enjoyably. Nobody snubs us. Araminta takes me to one side and tells me she has been thinking about Freddie all morning, which is kind, and doesn't refer to any possible engagement of mine. The Earl and Countess shake my hand particularly warmly. Tables have been set up in the garden under the trees and we eat the usual fare: lobster salad, salmon mayonnaise, capons, a boar's head, ices, fruit and so forth. Mama recognizes in the display of wedding gifts a silver sugar shaker from Charity Carstairs which is the very one we gave her when she married last spring; she can tell from a small dent in the side. (The item is antique.) She says nothing to the FitzWilliams but mentions the fact to Letty Morgan, thus ensuring it will soon be widely known. It is disappointing when people fall below one's expectations, however low they might be to begin with – which is certainly the case with the inaptly-named Charity Carstairs.

*

Paris awaits… I had written a note to Captain Hughes-Hampton, telling him of our intentions, and this afternoon he called at the house. 'How long are you going to be away?' he asked impatiently, tapping his swordstick against his calf. Mama looked approving but I couldn't help recalling Julia's words. I am hardly in a position to judge him, however, with the secret shame of Ireland still engraved upon my heart. We probably deserve each other. I told him we are planning to stay for a week or two and he snorted, like an angry blond bull. On leaving, he muttered surreptitiously that life would be awfully dull without me, even though I never wanted to go anywhere or do anything, and that he hoped I wouldn't forget about him while I was away.

As one might have expected, Beth has not reacted to news of the forthcoming expedition with anything like enthusiasm. This evening she informed me she was in two minds about coming at all but, as she's always had a hankering to see Paris, she has graciously consented to join us. 'Well, thank you very much. How terrifically kind of you,' I said, although of course the irony passed over her head. She will tend to the Johnsons and myself, as she did in Ireland. No one is alluding to that particular excursion but I think it must have crossed Mrs Johnson's mind as she's been shooting me more of her significant looks. We shall be staying at Le Meurice, overlooking the Tuileries gardens: lodgings which I hope will meet with Beth's approval. She and Kate's maid, Hortense, will be sharing a room in the basement. I remarked that if the Meurice is good enough for Queen Victoria it should be good enough for her. And there are always plenty of English people staying there so Mrs Johnson will have someone to talk to.

I must be back in Mama's good books because she and Papa are covering my expenses, although I'm not in a position to order any gowns from Worth or Doucet unlike certain other members of the party. However the prospect of wandering about Paris, alone and anonymous, is balm to my wounded soul. We shall be missing Madame Cellini's 'at home' in Brook Street but I was in two minds about going anyway.

Paris

Saturday June 17^{*th*}
We are here! And heady, heavenly France is already casting its spell. I am determined not to forget a single moment but to write my diary religiously every day.

The journey: This morning, Kate, the Johnsons and I take the boat train from Victoria, with Beth and Hortense travelling together further down the train. (The Duxfords will be joining us a few days later as Charlotte and her mother have social obligations in London.) There are no empty first-class carriages so we select one occupied by two respectable elderly women in lace caps. We are later joined by the most exotic dandy of a Frenchman: silky-haired and moustachioed, dressed in a suit of pale lilac with a gold brocade waistcoat and a bunch of wilting violets in his buttonhole. (He does not speak but we hardly need the odour of exotic tobacco overlaid with eau-de-cologne to confirm his nationality.) The ladies regard him suspiciously as, oblivious of our stares, he spends some minutes brushing the seat with a white linen handkerchief before sitting down, arranging one leg carefully over the other so as not to disturb the crease in his trousers, and closing his eyes. I catch Julia's eye and try not to giggle. Then with a shriek of the whistle, a blast of steam and a grinding of mighty cogs and levers, we are off.

Train travel reminds me of Ireland and my frame of mind as we travelled north by rail to Holyhead. I was mad then, deluded and alone in my confusion; now I am a sadder but wiser person, I hope, with friends around me. My burden of ignominy will always be with me, an albatross around my neck, yet perhaps in time I shall be able to forgive myself even if it is impossible to forget. I still wake up in the small hours, wondering how I could ever have acted in such a reckless fashion. The only answer that has come thus far is that he – the smooth-tongued Irish charmer – is so practised in deception he can make anyone do exactly as he pleases: whether it be investing in his crackpot scheme or falling in love. It wouldn't surprise me to learn he'd trained in the art of hypnosis. He must have deemed me useful for his purposes and so took advantage of my sweet and trusting nature. That is what hurts as much as anything: the thought of such innocence being callously destroyed, never to return.

Eugenie's Story

But enough of the past: onward now, into the future! We are speeding away from the long London streets of terraced houses, their red roofs and chimney stacks shimmering in the heat, away from soot-speckled laundry flapping in back gardens and hoardings on grimy walls advertising Sunlight Soap. Before long we have reached the orchards and oast houses of my beautiful, beloved Kent: the garden of England. It is comforting to picture the magical world of Swallowcliffe only a few miles away behind these wooded hills. Perhaps even now Papa is contemplating another row of bricks standing proudly atop his wall. I feel a sudden pang of missing him and send my love through the air as we sweep on towards the coast. Mrs Johnson has struck up conversation with the spinsters. They are leaving the train at Folkestone and seem appalled to hear we are travelling on to Paris. 'Because of the bombs, of course,' they chorus in response to Mrs Johnson's alarmed enquiry. 'Surely you've heard about those terrible anarchists, blowing up the restaurant and a police station?' The dozing Frenchman opens one eye, casting a supercilious glance at us before closing it again without deigning to comment. It is left to me to reassure Mrs Johnson and the mob caps that while it's true a couple of bombs were set off in Paris last year, those responsible have been brought to justice and the city is perfectly safe once more. The spinsters are not convinced. 'They're planning to put acid in the water supply,' confides one. Mrs Johnson's jaw sets resolutely; it would take more than a couple of anarchists to frighten *her*! One might think she were anticipating such an encounter with some relish.

The landscape opens out, becoming less a cozy green patchwork blanket tucked around trees and hedgerows than a threadbare cloak tossed over the stony ground. We are nearing Folkestone and gradually descend towards the port, where the train stops. The ladies collect their carpet bags and wish us a safe onward journey in the manner of those bidding farewell to Dr Livingstone *en route* to darkest Africa. We partake of some refreshment in the dining room of the Royal George Hotel while waiting for the steamer. Mindful of the sea crossing that is to come, Julia and I eat very little. Kate is not hungry either; in fact she seems generally preoccupied. I hope she isn't worried by those silly rumours but perhaps she is more concerned about leaving Edward behind in London, free to get up to all kinds of mischief. The Frenchman eyes the pork pies and pallid sausages on the plates of those around him before ordering a single orange, which he proceeds to peel with his own tiny pearl-handled knife and eat, segment by meticulous segment, dabbing at his mouth with another handkerchief. (At least, I hope it's another handkerchief and not the one he employed to brush his seat.) And then it is time to board the boat and set our faces towards France.

'All right, my dear?' Mrs Johnson enquires discreetly, joining me at the rail as I survey the calm blue water: so much more benign than the choppy Irish Sea.

'Perfectly well, thank you,' I assure her, and she nods, although she continues to watch me from a nearby seat while pretending to read a newspaper. I can't help but think how my story might have ended on that previous awful journey, and the recollection casts a shadow over this sunny day. How I envy Mrs Johnson, and others like her, who see everything in black-and-white and are not at the mercy of passionate emotions…

I notice Kate taking the air and make my way over to join her. When I remark on her apparent thoughtfulness, she asks me whether I remember that day we looked at the derelict barn together. It turns out she is pressing ahead with her plan for the almshouses; her father is going to provide funds and Mrs Johnson is also making a contribution. I still have grave misgivings about the whole idea but I suppose now Edward is hardly in a position to object. This independence of spirit can only deepen the gulf between the two of them, however, which is wide enough already. I feel a shiver of apprehension, realizing afresh how vital it is to choose the right person with whom to spend one's life. Still, Paris will give me valuable time to reflect.

Having suffered only moderately from sea-sickness and spent most of the voyage on deck, in a matter of hours I see the French coast hove into view, drawing steadily closer until, after much running about by blue-trousered sailors and grinding of the piston rods, accompanied by deafening blasts on the ship's horn and a shower of Gallic exclamation, we dock at Boulogne. Beth and Hortense attend to the checking of our trunks and suitcases in the customs' house while we take refreshment, suddenly ravenous after being buffeted about by the sea breezes. The dining hall is somewhat rough and ready, with long communal tables and little service to speak of, but oh, the food! Tawny roast chickens, plump and juicy with flavour; crusty baguettes of feather-light bread; little honey sponge cakes; even the carafes of wine and brandy are imbued with Continental glamour. France has its own exotic, characteristic smell: pungent tobacco smoke overlaid with notes of garlic, wine, that musky eau-de-cologne French women seem to love, and the merest whiff of drains. I see Julia's eyes widen as she gazes about. 'Wait till we reach Paris,' I tell her. 'This is only the beginning.'

Another train journey follows, enlivened by passing through French hamlets, French horses in the fields lifting their heads to watch as we speed by and French dogs wandering down dusty French lanes. Gradually the farms diminish and the houses increase until we see factories and tall chimneys on the horizon, and soon nobody bothers to look up at a train because we are approaching the city, where everyone is absorbed in their own mysteriously enchanting life. We spill out on to the platform at the Gare du Nord and, with much gesticulating and shouting from porters, are crammed into a cab which bears us jolting through the busy streets. Beth and Hortense follow in another with the luggage. Lamps are starting to be lit in the pavement cafés as elegantly-dressed couples hurry past on their way to the opera or the theatre, or maybe to dine. (It would seem not everyone of note has left for the coast.) The roads widen as we approach the magnificent Louvre and Tuileries gardens, and finally we are decanted into the blessed peace of the Meurice, its marble floors shining and its thick curtains drawn against a velvety blue Parisian evening, sprinkled with stars.

*

And now I am too tired to write any more; a canopied bed, piled high with pillows and cushions, beckons me from across the room. This magical city will still be here in the morning, waiting for us to explore at our leisure.

Thursday, June 22nd
Well, as you can see, I haven't managed to write this journal every day. I am too busy living my life to record it in fine detail; broad brush strokes will have to suffice. We are comfortably settled in the marvellous Meurice: a loosely-assembled but congenial party among whom several unexpected alliances are already being formed.

Firstly the Duxfords appeared: Charlotte and her mother, to attend to the wedding gown, and Henry, to moon after me. I did wonder whether my relations with Charlotte might be a little strained but she broached the subject herself, finding me lingering alone over breakfast one morning (the hotel has bacon sent over from Fortnums' for English guests, and its croissants are heavenly). She said she thought there might have been a particular friendliness between myself and Lord McGillie and hoped I wasn't harbouring any hard feelings on account of their subsequent engagement. I was able to reassure her quite sincerely the friendliness had all been on His Lordship's part, not mine, and that I wished her only well.

Poor Charlotte! Her eyes have taken on a glassy stare, like those of a rabbit in the beam of a poacher's lantern. I think she can't quite believe what has happened, but now her mother has the bit between her teeth, there can be no turning back. For some extraordinary reason the wedding is to be held

Eugenie's Story

in November, that most miserable of months (and in Scotland, too!), so presumably the guests will be in furs and Charlotte will be frozen half to death. One might almost feel sorry for her. Lady Duxford, triumphant, talks of nothing but the splendours of Monkton Abbey; apparently the old Earl is fading fast so Charlotte may find herself installed there sooner rather than later. Henry announces himself charmed by Paris and has taken to going about in a wide-brimmed matador's hat with a sketchbook under one arm. He and Mrs Johnson have interminable discussions about the future of Europe compared to the future of America.

My brother Rory has also joined us for a few days. He says there's nothing much going on in London (which I find hard to believe), and he can't bear to think of us all in the Meurice, his favourite hotel, without him. He's taken it upon himself to cheer up Kate and seems to be succeeding. She has perked up sufficiently to organize a variety of excursions for those in our group not taken up with artistic pursuits or shopping: a trip by charabanc to the Bois de Boulogne, bicycle rides through the Luxembourg gardens, a visit to the Comédie-Française and so on. Plum has become her lieutenant in this, since he seems to know everyone in Paris there is to be known and to have done everything that is worth doing, so he is full of useful advice. He is staying in the Meurice with us because the château is too full of ghosts, he says, and will only make him miserable. However he has promised to show us around the house before we leave. It is to the north of Paris apparently, on the edge of a forest. Although he is here to carry out a sad duty, his spirits seem to be rallying a little and I feel this change of scene is doing him good, too.

Out of all of us, Julia seems the most overwhelmed by the city. She spent some time lying on my bed last night, staring up at the ceiling while she tried to explain. 'There's something about the beauty of it that makes me want to cry. The light on the river, the boulevards and squares, the little winding streets in Montmartre – they speak to my very soul. And the people! Don't you think they live life more intensely than we do, Genie? Even that old lady selling flowers on the street corner looks like a gypsy queen. Simply being here makes me feel so interesting. And you seem back to your old self, more or less.'

My old self! Alas, that has gone, never to return. But, pressed by Julia to describe the effect the city has had on me, I decided the rallying cry of the French Revolution we had seen painted on a wall in Boulogne – *liberté, égalité, fraternité* – sums up my present state of mind. Here I am certainly liberated, free from the prying eyes of gossips and the expectations of my peers. As for *égalité,* why, in my gown from Madame Angeline and a cleverly trimmed hat, I like to think I am the equal of any Parisienne strolling down the Champs Elysées! And in terms of fraternity, there is a definite bond between we fellow travellers in these foreign parts, both those in our small party and the wider circle of British expatriates to whom we nod discreetly over our breakfast bacon and eggs.

I am, however, a little worried that the Johnsons have let Paris go to their heads. They are in danger of becoming recklessly Bohemian, in character rather than merely costume (unlike solid Henry in his matador hat). Heaven knows where that will lead. For one thing, they travel all over the city by means of the Métro, which is even noisier and smellier than London's Underground system. And despite my protestations to the elderly ladies on the train, Paris is not quite as tranquil as we had thought. Although there is no sign of any anarchist activity, a confrontation between some students and policemen in the Latin Quarter a few days before we arrived resulted in the death of one young man, and the trouble is still continuing. I have made Julia promise not to go anywhere near that area but I fear she and her mother may stumble across it by mistake; they seem to have only the vaguest idea of their whereabouts at any given time and find their way by luck rather than judgement. No, there are dangerous currents washing through these boulevards and I am worried the Johnsons may be swept up in them.

They have embraced the life of the *flâneur* a little too enthusiastically in my opinion, strolling about the city as if it belonged to them.

Secondly, Julia seems to be paying even less attention to her toilette than usual. She now refuses to wear a corset at night, although I have strongly recommended the habit, so Beth is hard put to lace her up sufficiently tightly in the morning. I know this because I have witnessed their titanic struggle. Just a little discipline in this matter would make all the difference, and show off Julia's gowns to their best advantage. *Il faut souffrir pour être belle*, as the French say, and any initial discomfort soon passes. She claims to sleep better now but I fear she may become fat and sluggish.

Both the Johnsons also seem to have become obsessed with art and, more alarmingly, with the artists who produce it. Mrs Johnson has fallen into the clutches of a certain Chester Knowles, whom she met in the hotel lobby: an American settled in Paris who acts as agent for several of the Impressionist painters and general arbiter of taste in artistic matters. As far as I can see, the only qualifications he possesses for this role are an obsequious manner and an intimate knowledge of the cafés in Montmartre, but Mrs Johnson won't hear a word said against him. He is a weaselly little fellow with a goatee beard and a curiously high-pitched voice. Through his auspices, however, Mrs Johnson has already purchased three pictures: a landscape by Monet (or the 'grand pappy of Impressionism', as Mr Knowles calls him), the portrait of a particularly unappealing, sulky child by an American lady whose name I forget, and worst of all, a work by the '*sauvage*' Gauguin, which has to be the crudest thing I have ever seen – all flat shapes in ugly clashing colours. I could have painted it myself had the urge to create something truly hideous possessed me, which thankfully so far it has not.

What Mr Johnson will say when he learns his wife has been wasting money in such spectacular fashion, I dread to think; these paintings are not cheap, despite being so horrid and generally derided by the *cognoscenti*. Luckily most of the Impressionists are currently daubing away at the seaside or in a field somewhere but Mr Knowles is threatening to introduce Mrs Johnson to some of the few still remaining in the city. (Mercifully this does not include Gauguin, currently in self-imposed exile on a South Sea island where he is doubtless churning out more horrors.) I have grave reservations about the whole matter. While I love the Johnsons dearly, they are somewhat naïve and vulnerable to being preyed upon by unscrupulous types. I shall do my best to protect them from exploitation but I cannot follow their every step.

Lastly, to complete my burden of worry, Beth is also a cause for concern. She is definitely up to something although I don't know exactly what. My suspicions were first alerted when I came across her puzzling over a copy of *Le Figaro*, and she informed me she is trying to improve her French. Now why would she want to do that? Apparently she had already acquired some basic vocabulary in England by means of a book from the lending library, and has been conversing with Hortense to improve her accent. The Johnsons have been taking her around the city with them and I gather she has been exploring further afield on her afternoons off; Julia said she had been to the Bois de Boulogne and highly recommended a trip there. Indeed! And yesterday Kate, Mrs Johnson and I were strolling through the Tuileries gardens after a visit to the Orangerie when I glimpsed her scurrying along the Rue de Rivoli in the company of a woman I did not recognize; they were too far away to see properly but it certainly wasn't Hortense. When I asked her that evening how she had spent the afternoon, she was evasive. A furtive look has replaced her vacant expression and occasionally there is a defiant note to her voice which I do not like at all. I have made it clear that her conduct reflects on our whole party, and that I don't want her associating with undesirables or otherwise bringing our family into disrepute. She muttered something under her breath and declined to repeat it, which I'm afraid is typical of her current behaviour.

Yet I must not give the impression that life

here is one of unalloyed anxiety. We are having some lovely times! To quote but one example, yesterday we went with the Duke to the salon of Madame Gallifrète: in her prime a leading light of Parisian society and still beautiful although a little absent-minded. We had nothing to drink and her cakes were stale but the conversation was most stimulating. When she remarked that twenty Impressionists were not worth one properly-trained academician from the Ecole des Beaux Arts, I agreed whole-heartedly. (Luckily Julia and her mother were not there to embarrass us with a different view.) In a hundred years' time no one will remember Monet, Degas or Gauguin and their humdrum paintings but the epic works of Duran, Détaille and Meissonier will still be widely admired.

Some other vignettes from our Parisian life:
We all dine together one evening at Napolitain, a restaurant recommended by Plum. I would never do such a thing in London but here it seems perfectly acceptable. At the next table a vivacious girl in exquisite emeralds catches my eye. The Duke tells me she is a dancer over whom a duel has recently been fought and that the jewels were given to her by an admirer, earning him the right to drink champagne from her slipper. Too thrilling!

In the gardens of the Palais-Royal, I walk past a young man dressed from head to toe in dazzling white, leading a lion cub on a golden chain.

We catch a glimpse of the legendary Sarah Bernhardt, striding energetically down the Avenue de l'Opéra in pantaloons and a black velvet cloak. She is terrifically thin. Plum knows her well (of course) and is certain she would have invited us to her *appartement* on the Boulevard Pereire, but for the fact she is rehearsing a new play. Unfortunately she is not currently appearing in one so we cannot see her on stage either.

Julia returns from a nearby street market with a sheaf of lavender for my dressing table, wrapped in pink tissue paper tied with a blue ribbon. That inimitable French chic...

Which reminds me: most remarkably of all, the skin on my hands is as soft as that of a baby! Not the slightest trace of eczema to be seen. There is a lesson here, and when I have a little time to spare I shall try to work out what it is. Just now, however, my hand is tired from writing and my head from thinking. And so, to bed!

Saturday June 24th

Captain HH has written to me twice; he doesn't have a great deal of news but always finishes by asking when we are coming home. I think if it were up to the Johnsons, we should be here for the duration. I am becoming increasingly worried about Julia. She is having her portrait painted by an intense young man called Jean-Luc Bruyère who comes highly recommended by Chester Knowles. That alone is enough to damn him in my eyes. This swarthy fellow usually turns up at the Meurice but yesterday Julia and her mother visited his studio in Montmartre, where apparently 'the light is better' (a likely story). It all seems most unsuitable. I observed one of their sittings and for every minute he spends actually painting Julia, he must spend ten more staring at her.

'Well, of course,' she protested when I remarked on this. 'He has to take a proper look at me, otherwise how would he know what to paint?' I believe he could do so in a less obvious manner, however; his expression is most disconcerting. He has little sharp teeth, like a wolf, and surprisingly pink lips hidden in the depths of a bushy black beard. In fact, I wouldn't be at all surprised if he turned out to be one of those anarchists intent on bringing Paris to its knees. I asked Julia whether they talk during these painting sessions and if so what they say, but she says he doesn't speak very good English. That is one blessing at least.

I have, however, come up with the most wonderful idea. I think Julia and my brother Rory are ideally suited. They have similarly happy-go-lucky characters and seem to get along terrifically well. Only yesterday I came across them laughing together over a drawing in *La Revue Blanche*, a new magazine that seems to be the *dernier cri* in modernity. I've begun to extol Rory's virtues in Julia's hearing, which isn't difficult as he is so funny and charming, and perhaps the germ of an idea is already beginning to grow in her mind. How splendid it would be if they were to marry and she became part of my family for ever! I am trying not to let this fancy run away with me (as admittedly is my wont) but it is so obviously the ideal course of action for all concerned. Julia, who although adorable is not a ravishing beauty, would gain a handsome husband, and Rory would have a doting wife who could buy them a lovely house somewhere.

Charlotte Duxford still looks wistfully at Rory but he was always out of her reach, and now she has made her bed so she must lie on it. She and her mother are returning to London on Tuesday as the wedding gown has been ordered and measurements taken. (She is slender but has a tendency to stoop.) Chester Knowles now has Henry in his clutches, however, and has been telling him about the village of Giverny, where Monet lives and where apparently there is quite an artists' colony gathered around him. Henry is determined to visit the place and no doubt would like the rest of us to decamp there, but I have not yet exhausted the delights of Paris. Besides, the Duke has promised to show us round the château on Thursday.

I think about the Captain sometimes but to be honest he is less present in my mind than he probably ought to be, which is worrying. I find it hard to recall what he looks like. Only small details stand out: the way his neck bulges over his shirt collar for example, or the habit he has of briskly pulling at his cuffs as if settling down to business. Yet knowing he is waiting for my return gives me a welcome sense of security. I shall probably agree to marry him in due course. Paris is deliciously exciting but I detect a note of decadence beneath its polished surface; one cannot live on rum babas for ever.

Monday June 26th

Well, I knew it. I always thought Beth was a snake in the grass and events have proved me right – although even I am surprised by the extent of her deception. And the worst of it is, she has created a rift between Julia and me that may never be healed.

Yesterday afternoon, the Johnsons and I went to explore Montmartre. It is already one of their favourite places, 'where anyone who cares about art or literature or poetry gathers in the local café to exchange ideas,' according to Julia. I had not been before and this description filled me with a certain amount of trepidation, as you might imagine, but actually at first sight the quartier seems charming. Narrow cobbled streets wind their way up the hill to the magnificent church at its summit: magnificent even though construction is not yet finished. We walked about the gardens, marvelling at the view of Paris spread out beneath us. In one direction we could see as far as the menacing iron elevations of the Eiffel Tower (which everyone considers terrifically ugly) and the golden dome of Les Invalides, sparkling in the sun; slightly nearer at hand we could spy Nôtre Dame, adrift on its island in the Seine. Sightseeing is exhausting although one doesn't actually do very much, and after an hour or so we were ready to descend.

On the way down, Julia pointed out Monsieur Bruyère's studio, which certainly looks dingy enough to qualify as an artist's garret. I don't believe any natural light can breach those high walls but Julia says there is a skylight at the back of the building. Tall houses lean close together across the streets, blocking out the sun. 'Why,' I remarked, 'if there are any other artists or poets living here, they won't need to find a café to exchange ideas – they can simply lean out of an upstairs window to chat to each other!' We laughed gaily at this; a poignant memory now, as I wonder whether Julia will ever appreciate one of my witticisms again.

She and her mother were walking just in front of me when suddenly, through the open doorway of a pavement café, I glimpsed a hat I recognized: grey straw, trimmed with a floppy white cabbage rose. I stopped dead, turned to stone. Beth was inside, sitting at a table with another person whom I took at first to be a man. But it was worse than that. Her companion was none other than – Mrs Thompson's assistant, Miss Pratt! Throwing back her head to laugh in the most disgustingly vulgar manner, her

Eugenie's Story

hair cropped short with an unforgiving fringe and NO HAT. She was wearing a shirt and tie with a masculine jacket over the sort of bicycling bloomers sported by Harriet and Miss Habershon, which was why I had at first mistaken her gender. But it was definitely her: I'd know those teeth anywhere. There was a carafe of red wine on the table between them and Miss Pratt, at least, had a glass from which she was drinking; I couldn't tell about Beth. It was the most disturbing sight. I stood in the road, transfixed, until finally coming to my senses and hurrying on before they could spot me in return. There was no point making a scene there and then. I had to collect my thoughts and decide how to approach the situation.

Julia sensed there was something wrong as we made our way back to the hotel by means of the Impériale, an omnibus drawn by three huge grey horses that regularly thunders through the wider Parisian streets. (The Johnsons consider it more 'picturesque' than a hansom cab; it is certainly more uncomfortable.) When we were alone together in Julia's room, I explained what had happened as briefly as possible. She didn't seem to understand. 'But Beth has the afternoon off,' she said. 'Why shouldn't she meet her friend?'

I couldn't bring myself to describe Miss Pratt's appearance: it was too distressing and Julia might not have understood the implications, being a year younger than I and more innocent. Leaving that aside, however, surely it was obvious we couldn't tolerate a servant behaving in such a manner. Drinking wine, in broad daylight, in a public place? Or at least, sitting in the company of someone drinking wine, which is almost as bad; someone who has clearly been corrupted by what I can now see is the febrile atmosphere of Montmartre, where for every idealistic poet or artist there is a pathetic *clochard* in the café, hunched over his (or her) glass of absinthe. We can't be attended to by a person who considers such conduct acceptable. And the deception of it! Why hadn't Beth told me Miss Pratt was in Paris?

I wonder what exactly that crafty young woman is doing here. She cannot still be in Mrs Thompson's employment, surely. Either that or Mrs Thompson does not know what an odd-looking character she has become: hardly the best advertisement for Madame Angeline's frothy creations. Remembering that we had received Miss Pratt at Swallowcliffe, and that she had given me such intimate attention, was enough to make my flesh crawl. Come to think of it, she must have been the person I saw in Beth's company walking along the Rue de Rivoli the other day. I had no idea they were such friends.

'Oh, I did,' Julia said airily. 'Beth was at needlework school with Miss Pratt. She told me so that time we went to Madame Angeline's.'

It was galling to be given information about my own maid by a person who has known her only a matter of months. 'Be that as it may, we have been sadly let down,' I said, 'and Beth will have to go. I'm sure the hotel can find us another maid.'

Unfortunately Julia did not agree. We had a spirited conversation about the rights and wrongs of the case and some forthright opinions were exchanged which I think she may now regret. I have come to the conclusion, based on personal observation, that Americans have no idea how to treat servants. For once in my life I missed Mama; she would have agreed with me, I'm sure, and given Beth her cards without a moment's hesitation.

I tossed and turned all night, and waited in a state of some anxiety this morning for Beth to appear. The interview was more upsetting than I could ever have imagined. The girl was not at all abashed to learn she had been found out; *au contraire*, she looked me straight in the eye and said she had a right to enjoy herself as much as anyone. The bare-faced cheek! And the ingratitude! Having been brought to Paris and accommodated in the best hotel, this is how she repays us. I knew then there was no point trying to reason with her and said she would have to leave our household as soon as we were back on English shores. (This was the compromise I had devised to assuage Julia. For myself, I would have dismissed her straight away to sink or swim in France as best she could.) Yet even this kindness was thrown back at me. She tore off her cap and flung it down, declaring she couldn't bear to 'bow and scrape' a second longer but would leave right away. She'd 'had enough of my ways,' apparently, which she said were enough to try the patience of a saint. And with that she turned her broad back on me and marched out, her shoulders rigid with unjustified indignation: a most unedifying spectacle altogether.

It took some time for my anger to subside into resigned disappointment. To be addressed so rudely by someone whom I have nurtured and trained from the most unpromising of beginnings was almost beyond belief. Well, I decided, at least it proves I was right all along and Julia wrong to give Bessie the benefit of the doubt. (I can no longer think of her as Beth: she does not deserve it.) When I went to Julia's room to tell her what had happened, however, I learned the girl had already gone running to tell the Johnsons her side of the story, and that I was expected to account for *my* actions in dismissing her! What else was I meant to have done, might I ask? The fact she will have no reference and no wages for the month is entirely her own fault.

I am extremely upset by the whole affair, and now I have to find another maid acceptable to Julia, Mrs Johnson and myself, when Julia is so cool towards me and won't lift a finger to help. I may have had enough of Paris; it is a corrupt and dangerous place which is enough to unsettle anybody. I think I shall go home on Friday, after visiting the château, and if I have found a nice quiet French girl by then, I shall take her with me. The Johnsons will just have to fend for themselves. Yes, I shall go home and marry Captain Hughes-Hampton, who is a respectable English gentleman, and that will show Julia what I think of her opinions.

Tuesday June 27th
A fairly uneventful morning so far. Bessie has gone, I believe, but Hortense informed me she has left a couple of dresses behind. On investigation they turned out to be two old frocks I'd once given her, minus the lace collars and cuffs which had been snipped off. She might as well have slapped me in the face. Rory has returned to England and the regiment — to Julia's apparent indifference, alas, although I hardly care about that now — Kate is in a bad mood, the Duke is occupied with his château, Henry Duxford is arranging the trip to Giverny and the Johnsons have gone to Montmartre. Perhaps even now they are sitting in a café, drinking wine and laughing at my outdated notions of respectability.

Later. O, dear Lord — smite me down for ever having written such a thing! Had I not resolved to let this record stand for posterity, I should tear out the page. It was only the upset with Bessie that prompted such bitterness. Dear sweet Julia, and her indomitable mother! The thought of them brings tears to my eyes.

    I cannot bring myself to continue. Kate needs me. She is waiting for news downstairs in the lobby, frantic with anxiety. All we know is that a bomb has exploded in Montmartre and that the Johnsons, who were due back several hours ago, have not yet returned. Henry has told us to stay in the hotel and gone to the area to find out what he can. I fear the worst and am sick with dread. If anything has happened to them, I shall never, ever forgive myself.

Eugenie's Story

Thursday June 29th
How long ago those terrible hours seem now! I remember sitting helplessly with Kate in the lobby of the Meurice, starting up at every disturbance in the street outside: running footsteps, the cry of a newspaper boy, clattering hooves as a platoon of *gendarmes* trotted past. Our nerves were stretched to breaking point. Catching sight of Chester Knowles emerging from the elevator, I set upon him, beating his chest with my fists and declaring it was all his fault the Johnsons had gone to Montmartre in the first place; he should never have encouraged them to frequent such a place or consort with such people. In my mind's eye I could see Julia and her mother held hostage by the dastardly Jean-Luc Bruyère, or lying unconscious in the street, their blood flowing across the cobblestones. The hotel manager himself tried to calm me down with a medicinal brandy, but the bottle only reminded me of Mrs Johnson and her hip flask, and I gave way to floods of tears. Kate urged me to rest in my room but I would not leave her waiting there alone. My distress, great as it was, must have been nothing compared to hers; I could not abandon her.

The two of us were sitting together, therefore, when marching into the hotel lobby came – Bessie! Through the main door, bold as brass. I drew myself up, about to tell her she had no business setting foot in this establishment any longer, but she forestalled me. 'It's all right, Ma'am,' she said, laying a hand on my arm, 'I've come with good news. I've seen Miss Julia and Mrs Johnson, and they're perfectly all right. They're safe! You don't need to worry no more.'

Kate and I needed a few seconds to take in the meaning of her words (double negatives don't help), but she repeated her message again until we understood. She had come across the Johnsons in Montmartre, among the crowd that had assembled to help and search for loved ones at the scene of the explosion, and they were unharmed. 'They're with some painter chappy,' she told us, 'so they can't come back quite yet, but I said I'd bring you a message. I'm sure they'll be home as soon as ever they can.'

Oh, the relief! Kate hugged Bessie, thanking her over and over again, and I was also most grateful. There was of course a little awkwardness between us, considering how we'd last parted, but I had to admit it was kind of the girl to put us out of our misery. A moment or so after she had left, a sudden impulse made me follow her out of the hotel. I saw her turning a corner at the end of the street and called for her to stop.

'May I offer you some money for the journey, and your trouble?' I asked when we were face to face. She said Mrs Johnson had already done so, however.

There we stood, the two of us: from different classes, to be sure, but both Englishwomen in a foreign city at the mercy of forces beyond our control. 'How is your friend, Miss Pratt?' I asked. 'I hope she hasn't been caught up in this terrible business.'

'Bless you, Miss,' she said. 'No, we're both all right. It's a dreadful thing, though – rubble and all sorts blocking the road.'

We would probably never see each other again, and I suddenly found myself surprisingly concerned for her welfare. I asked her whether she had found another position. 'No, Ma'am,' she said. 'I've had enough of service. Me and Miss Pratt have set up in business together, making costumes for the dancers at the Folies Bergère. We're renting a workshop in Montmartre with rooms above. It's only a couple of streets away from where the bomb went off but no damage done, thank goodness.'

The phrase 'going to hell in a handcart' crossed my mind, but I managed not to utter it out loud and merely wished her well for the future. Given the limitations of her character and education, I suppose one cannot judge the girl too harshly. She was always more of a Bessie than a Beth at heart, I realized on the way back to the hotel, and one can only do so much to elevate a person beyond his or her natural level.

*

Kate and I composed ourselves to wait for the Johnsons in a calmer frame of mind, knowing they

Swallowcliffe Hall

would eventually be returning. And after an hour or so, the revolving brass doors of the Meurice turned again and out spilled... Julia. Pale-faced and shocked, but safe and sound. Another revolution and her mother was delivered to us, followed after another by Henry, grinning from ear to ear. I could have thrown my arms around his neck and kissed him, except for the fact I was busy embracing Julia, and she was hugging me back in a manner that told me all was forgiven. Dear Henry: he might not be the most exciting person in the world but one can always rely on him. (And as a matter of fact he's looking much more dashing and debonair these days, thanks to Paris.) Mrs Johnson also seemed delighted to see me. Any lingering reservations on either side – hers at the sincerity of my repentance, mine at her unshakeable self-righteousness – had been swept away by the crisis and we greeted each other as the dear friends we have since remained.

When we had all recovered a little, the Johnsons told us their story. They had heard the explosion from Monsieur Bruyère's studio. He had immediately rushed out to investigate, being concerned about his wife who was at work in a nearby *pâtisserie*. (Imagine him being married, and to someone so ordinary! You'd think she could have persuaded him to shave off that dreadful beard.) He had later returned to the house in such a terrible state of agitation (trembling and weeping real tears, Julia said) that the Johnsons felt they couldn't leave him. The bomb, which people were saying was indeed the work of anarchists, had gone off near the aforementioned *pâtisserie*, in a café where Madame Bruyère often called to deliver tarts and pastries on the way home when her work was over. Why the anarchists should have chosen such a place to leave their evil device, when the area is seething with sympathizers, is beyond me; I suspect they are not over-burdened with intelligence.

Anyway, Monsieur Bruyère found out his wife had indeed left for the café that afternoon with her basket of baked goods. He had gone there but taken one look at the ruined building and lost his head, running home in hysterics – far too terrified of what he might find to join those searching through the rubble. Urging him to stay strong, the Johnsons had sallied forth, supporting him between them. They discovered the front of the restaurant had been almost completely destroyed but the back was intact, and luckily only a waiter had been killed as it was not a particularly busy time of day. And as they were inspecting the scene, Madame Bruyère had suddenly appeared and flung herself into her husband's arms, to cries of joy on every side! A chance meeting had delayed her in the street so she hadn't yet reached the café when the bomb went off. She had been sheltering in the cellar of a neighbour's house, believing an earthquake had struck the city and too afraid until then to venture outside.

For our part, the relief of finding out our friends were unharmed was exquisite, and Henry was delighted with himself for finding them amongst the crowd at the bombsite and bringing them safely home; it really was most touching. Plum had also rejoined us by now. On hearing the news of the Johnsons' narrow escape, he took everyone off for celebratory champagne followed by dinner in the hotel. (Hortense helped me change, while Julia and her mother seemed happy to look after each other.) Chester Knowles was included in the party and I noticed him looking at me warily. I smiled back distantly, trying to convey I was prepared to be sociable but my reservations still existed. It would do him no harm to know someone was looking after the Johnsons' interests, although I admit terror might have had led me to express myself more directly than usual during the height of the crisis.

'The odd thing is,' Mrs Johnson said as we were tucking into our *suprêmes de volailles*, 'those funny old ladies on the train were right, much as we scoffed at the time. It turns out Paris is rather a dangerous city after all.'

Henry and Mr Knowles immediately started talking about Giverny. They said it was a beautiful spot on the banks of the Seine, about fifty miles to the north-west of Paris: a farming hamlet which had so captivated Monet when he glimpsed it from the window of a passing train, that he immediately decided to move there. A small band of acolytes has gathered about him at a hotel in the village, where they spend all day painting and all evening discussing the fruits of their labours. 'Doesn't it sound splendid?' Henry asked rhetorically. 'And only this morning I received an answer from the hotel to my letter of enquiry, saying there are a few rooms available.'

It sounded frightfully dull to me but clearly no one else held the same view so I bit my tongue. The Johnsons were just declaring they should like to set off at the earliest opportunity – Monsieur Bruyère's portrait of Julia being almost finished – when I caught sight of Plum's crestfallen face. 'What about our visit to the château?' I reminded the others. 'We can't possibly miss that!'

After much deliberation it was decided that the Johnsons and Henry would leave for Giverny the next morning, while Kate and I visited Plum's château with him as planned, joining the painting party the day after that. The Johnsons were anxious not to offend His Grace and made many apologies but I think he was probably relieved to have fewer people tramping around a house that was so clearly dear to his heart. He particularly wanted to show it to Kate and me, I think – or perhaps it was more that he especially wanted our company when he went there himself, because of the memories the house contained and his sadness at having to bid it farewell.

Mrs Johnson can be a little insensitive to 'thoughts that do lie too deep for tears,' in Wordsworth's memorable phrase. At any rate, the matter was settled to everyone's satisfaction, although Henry made a point of saying he hoped Kate and I would not delay our trip to Giverny any further as he knew how much we would love it there.

So the Johnsons and Henry were the first to leave the Meurice. I was sorry to see Julia go, having so recently thought I might have lost her for ever, but it wouldn't be long before we were reunited. This morning Kate, the Duke and I set off by train for the château, which lies about twenty-five miles to the south of Paris on the outskirts of a forest. I was too preoccupied on the journey to take much notice of the passing scenery because that morning I had received a letter from Captain Hughes-Hampton, ordering me to come home. He had read newspaper reports of the explosion and considered Paris far too dangerous a place for us to remain a moment longer. If I did not return immediately, he said, he would come and fetch me himself. No doubt I should have been glad he was concerned for my safety but this ultimatum only irritated me, and my irritation was in itself perplexing. Didn't I want to see him again? All would soon become clear, however.

We descended from the train at a small country station where a barouche, complete with a liveried coachman and footman in the Clarebourne colours of claret and grey, was waiting to take us to the Château Alma. The Duke had given us the impression it was little more than a decent-sized house, which is perhaps why the Johnsons were prepared to forgo the chance of a tour, so we were unprepared for the sight that greeted us around a corner of the long, winding drive. A miniature fairy-tale castle in grey stone rose up against the dark tangle of woods behind, complete with turrets, a huddle of silvery-tiled roofs and pale blue shutters at every window.

Kate and I were struck dumb. We could only gasp in amazement, uttering inarticulate cries of joy as further glories were revealed the closer we drew: the rearing stone horses of a mossy fountain, an overgrown avenue of cypress trees, an arbour smothered in tumbling jasmine. The forest was encroaching rapidly upon the house, which seemed in danger of being swallowed up entirely, but that only added to its charm. We might have stumbled upon Sleeping Beauty's enchanted palace. The Duke smiled at our enthusiasm and said he supposed the place *was* rather pretty.

'It's perfect!' I cried, climbing down from the barouche. 'How can you bear to let it go?' I saw a shadow cross his face and berated myself for my thoughtlessness. The château obviously reminded him of his wife; perhaps they'd thought they would be happy here and now only the ashes of those dreams remained.

The interior of the house was as exquisite as the outside, although its many empty rooms had the same poignant atmosphere of solitude and regret. The château might have been longing for visitors who would never come: for its grand four-poster beds to be slept in, for its tapestries and paintings to be admired, for friends to set the rafters of the cavernous dining hall ringing with chat and laughter. 'I make the servants remove all the dustsheets before I visit,' the Duke said, 'otherwise it is simply too sad.' He told us the house had been a wedding present from his wife's father. Originally built as a hunting lodge, it was later transformed into this romantic retreat for a homesick Italian *principessa* who had married into the French aristocracy.

Parts of the house date back to the sixteenth century; the walls are tremendously thick and the stone steps leading up the turret to a circular wood-panelled room at the top have been polished by generations of feet. We climbed up to admire the view and explored some of the musty bedrooms before descending again to the ground floor and its formal reception rooms: a large drawing room filled with Louis Quinze furniture overlooking the gardens, a library, a music room and the dining hall, complete with a huge inglenook fireplace. I guessed the kitchen and servants' quarters were tucked away behind the thick studded oak door. A butler and housekeeper with a couple of maids had been waiting for our arrival; outside I had noticed only one gardener, an elderly man swiping at a patch of grass with a scythe. It seemed a futile gesture.

'This house deserves to be full of life,' Plum said, echoing my own thoughts. 'I can't keep it locked up any longer, although I shall miss the place – the idea of it, at any rate, waiting quietly for me. Within these walls the rest of the world seems very far away.'

We were standing in the drawing room, looking out across the terrace to a raggedy lawn dotted with bushy box trees that must have once been neatly clipped. An involuntary sigh escaped my lips. My heart was suddenly bursting with such emotion, it made me feel faint. Everything in my life so far – losing first my mother and then darling Freddie, my struggles with Mama, my humiliation in Ireland, the fear that Julia might be torn away from me too – seemed designed to have brought me to this secluded, blissful spot, in this particular frame of mind. Here I could look at myself with a gentler eye, seeing through my mistakes to the loneliness that lay behind them and forgiving the foolish girl I had been then. A huge weight was lifted from my shoulders and tears of gratitude prickled at my eyes, which I had to hurriedly conceal with a handkerchief in the pretence of blowing my nose.

'My dear girl!' exclaimed the Duke in concern. 'Are you all right?' He pulled out a chair for me to sit down. Kate was inspecting portraits at the far end of the room so she was unaware of any disturbance but I didn't want to make a fuss. In fact I felt suddenly euphoric.

'I'm perfectly well, thank you,' I said, smiling radiantly through moist eyes. 'It's just, the house is so full of … I don't know – love, I suppose, and glimpses of what might have been.'

He said he knew exactly what I meant. 'I have been both happier and sadder here than anywhere else in the world. Somehow one's heart speaks particularly loudly in this place, or perhaps there is simply peace and solitude enough to hear it.'

I had to speak openly: there seemed to be no point in doing anything else. 'I have been trying to decide whether I should marry a particular person,' I confided. 'I've been thinking about it for weeks and still don't know if it's the right thing to do. How can one ever make up one's mind about such a thing?'

'Sometimes thinking isn't helpful,' he replied. 'You probably already know who is the right husband – indeed the only husband – for you. Let your heart tell you who he is. Imagine yourself in five years' time. Who is the person standing by your side through thick and thin, who makes you laugh, whose smile makes your spirits leap, whose arms will comfort you in troubled times? If you are quiet and still, his face may come to you.'

It was a lovely idea but try as I might to see an

image of my perfect helpmate, no vision came to me then; nor later, as we walked about the neglected gardens. Plum showed us the remains of a herb garden that had been planted years ago, of which only a bay tree and a few leggy rosemary bushes were left, with some ancient terracotta olive jars the Italian princess had brought from Italy lying abandoned amongst them. We ate lunch in a summerhouse there – bread, various cheeses and *saucisson sec* – then wandered back to the house for coffee, and for the Duke to have a final conversation with his staff.

There was nothing particular in my mind on the journey home either, nor earlier this evening as Kate's maid Hortense helped me change for dinner, in a rather perfunctory fashion, and pinned up my hair. (So annoying I should have had to dismiss Bessie just when she was beginning to be useful!) Yet as I perched for a moment on the window seat, thinking over what Plum had said, suddenly a face *did* come into my mind – quite out of the blue but with all the force of a train thundering down the track, blowing out steam and shrieking its whistle. The last face I would ever have expected to see, but one I immediately recognized as indescribably dear. The revelation stunned me for a moment, and then my heart became filled with such joy, I laughed out loud. Of course! How could I possibly have imagined marrying anyone else? It was the most extraordinary vision: as though a curtain had been drawn aside to disclose what had been right under my nose for months, if not years. I sat stock still, examining my newfound knowledge from every angle. So many times in my life when I had been unhappy and alone, this person had offered me a word of comfort, stretched out a helping hand which I had failed to appreciate.

I cannot yet bring myself to write his name in case this episode is destined to end in failure, like so many of my faltering attempts to find love. My journal is witness to various moments when I have acted rashly on impulse, and I'm determined not to make the same mistake again. I shall hug my secret close a little longer. However I have already written to Captain Hughes-Hampton, telling him I have no intention of returning to England and that there's no point in him coming to fetch me as, by the time he receives the letter, we will already have left Paris for the country. In fact it would be best if he put me out of his mind altogether, as I now realize we are completely unsuited and I could never make him happy. As I sealed the envelope, the narrowness of my escape made me shiver.

I have eaten a quiet dinner alone in my room. Now I must prepare for Giverny, and the rest of my life.

Giverny

Friday July 7ᵗʰ
We are staying at the Hôtel Baudy, which could hardly be more different from Le Meurice although it is just as wonderful in its own way. Formerly the village grocer's shop and bar, the odours of coffee, cheese, *pastis* and many other good things seem to have soaked into the very fabric of the building. It stands in the middle of the village, less than half a mile from Monet's house, quintessentially French with its pink stucco walls and grey shutters. Madame Baudy, the proprietress, has had extra bedrooms built to accommodate the dozens of visitors who have swamped the sleepy hamlet of Giverny since Monet settled here. They have come from all over the world to worship at the feet of their master; to paint, sculpt or write (sometimes all three!) in the beautiful Norman countryside and the many *ateliers* that have sprung up all over the village; to drink, feast and talk long into the night. Far from the intense and frankly

dreary-sounding place conjured up by Henry's description, the hotel is the epicentre of this revelry, a welcoming home to assorted eccentrics and *bons viveurs*. Most are American but there are a fair few Englishmen, a couple of Swedes and a kilted Scot who has brought his bagpipes with him – much to Mrs Johnson's delight.

Madame Baudy serves the best kind of peasant food: suckling pig roasted all day on a spit; hearty casseroles rich with red wine, garlic and herbs; all manner of cheeses unheard of in England; apple tarts the size of wagon wheels with cauldrons of thick yellow cream. The butter is the sweetest I have ever tasted, the coffee dark and rich, and we finish dinner every night with a small glass of calvados, the apple brandy for which this region is famous. The grocery still remains in business alongside the hotel but now it also sells Twining's tea imported from England, maple syrup and marshmallows for the Americans, and brushes, canvas and paints supplied by Foinet's in Paris for the artists.

It would be hard to imagine a more congenial spot to embrace both art and life itself. Painting is not compulsory; there are two tennis courts at the hotel and bicycles in the village, or one may simply wander through the marshy fields, threading one's way among the artists' white umbrellas that sprinkle the grass like mushrooms. Two tributaries of the Seine, the Rû and the Epte, trickle through this fertile valley, and one can see the larger river in the distance, bordered by cypress trees. Vineyards and orchards clothe the gentle slopes and everywhere there are flowers: flag irises and poppies growing wild; roses, lilies and a hundred other cultivated plants spilling out of the village gardens.

Everyone says that Monet's garden trumps them all. Mrs Johnson is desperate to meet him but has so far been unsuccessful, despite a letter of introduction from Mr Knowles (who thankfully has stayed in Paris rather than joining us here). I have a feeling his friendship with the great man may turn out to be somewhat exaggerated. Mrs Johnson walks past Monet's house at least twice a day in the hope he may suddenly rush out to invite her inside, but so far she has been unlucky. Perhaps if he learns she has already bought one of his paintings, and has seemingly inexhaustible funds to invest in more, he will change his mind.

So how do we occupy ourselves? Kate, Julia and Henry spend a great deal of time sketching in the valley and the hotel gardens. I'm at last becoming more proficient on a bicycle, and we have also taken a rowing boat on jaunts down the river for picnics among the willows. Kate is beginning to look a little happier. She has thrown herself into planning the almshouses at Stone Martin, which seems to be bringing her peace of mind as well as sharpening her resolution. Apart from these excursions, I must confess to whiling away the hours sitting under a parasol in the garden, daydreaming. It's hard to tell whether Giverny seems so wonderful because I am in love, or whether it is partly because of Giverny that I feel so blissfully happy. Never has a sky seemed so intensely blue, a river so crystal clear, leaves and grass so vibrantly green. Maybe Impressionism is not quite so absurd after all; there might be something to be said for painting daily scenes and humble objects rendered glorious by sunlight. Each morning is filled with the promise of joys to come: a smile from my beloved, a stroll with him through the water meadows, daydreams about the blissful life we will soon share.

As it happens, I am not the only one with such dreams in my head. Last night, when Julia and I were having one of our chats (which thankfully have resumed), she confessed that she and Henry Duxford have become very fond of each other, and she had accepted his proposal of marriage that very day. Henry Duxford! I was extremely surprised, I must confess, though I managed to hide it. 'I know you have your reservations about him,' Julia said, 'but in my opinion he's the sweetest, kindest man in the whole world and I love him with all my heart, so will you try to be happy for me?'

'But of course!' I cried, embracing her – and truly, I am. While Henry would not be my choice, he is an Englishman from a good family who are friends and neighbours of ours. 'Do you know,' I said, drawing back, 'I did once hope you might marry my brother Rory, but after him, Henry Duxford is the next best thing!'

'It's odd you should say that,' she replied, 'because Henry thought I had set my sights on Rory too! Which is ridiculous, because Rory's quite clearly in love with – ' And then she stopped, and wouldn't go on. It *was* rather a silly remark, because if Rory were in love with anyone of course I should know about it first. She quickly changed the subject, saying she had been in love with Henry for months but tried to hide it because she thought he was in love with me, while he was unsure of declaring himself to her, believing she was hankering after my brother. What knots we tie ourselves up in!

The reality of the situation, in my opinion, is that Henry realized I was in love with somebody else and finally accepted I would never be his, so turned his attentions elsewhere. (Of course I was too tactful to share this idea with Julia.) I had noticed she was looking particularly radiant but put it down to the magic of Giverny. It's true she and Henry were lately to be seen with their easels closer together than was strictly necessary, and that they usually contrived to sit next to each other at dinner, but I thought little of it at the time.

Apparently Henry had already asked Mrs Johnson for Julia's hand, given her father's absence, and Mrs J is 'over the moon' about the whole thing because she adores Henry almost as much as Julia. Lady Duxford will be overjoyed too. First her daughter snaffles a Scottish (soon-to-be) earl, then her son bags an American heiress! Thank goodness she and Charlotte are back in London or we would be in for more hours of trumpet-blowing. The plan is for Henry to return to America with the Johnsons in September for a month to meet her family, and they will marry there next spring. 'I'm fixing to order my wedding gown when we get back to Paris,' Julia told me, her eyes sparkling. 'Will you come with me, darling Genie? I shall need your advice. Or do you think I should go to Mrs Thompson instead?'

I was torn – not about advising Julia on her wedding gown, of course, which I was only too delighted to do, but about sharing my own news. My dear one wants to keep it a secret until he has asked Papa for my hand; he still thinks I may change my mind, no matter how many times I reassure him I've never been more certain of anything in my life. Yet how could I resist telling Julia, when we were alone together, and she was sitting there talking about wedding gowns? So, having sworn her to secrecy, I relayed the whole story. She in her turn was a little surprised by my choice but, after a moment's reflection, pronounced herself delighted – and so relieved I wasn't going to marry that 'awful Hughes-Hampton man'. I admitted she had been completely

Eugenie's Story

right; his very name is enough to induce a shiver of disquiet. This morning I received a letter from Mama, in which she says that according to what she has just heard from Lady Hughes-Hampton, I may have overplayed my hand in terms of appearing elusive. Yet I never made the Captain any promises. I feel a little apprehensive about his reaction to my letter, but with my darling beside me, I am protected from his anger.

*

This is how events unfolded. After we had been at Giverny a couple of days, Plum and I were lingering over a late breakfast. Monet had been sighted, striding over some distant field, so Mrs Johnson and Kate had set off in hot pursuit in the hope of seeing him at work. Henry and Julia were playing tennis with a couple of American artists; calls and laughter drifted over occasionally from the court. I became suddenly filled with blissful contentment, like a cat basking in the sun. There was nowhere I would rather have been sitting, and no one with whom I would sooner have shared that wonderful morning.

The Duke smiled at me over his coffee cup. 'You look so happy, Eugenie, and I'm glad to see it. I've been tormented by the thought some action of mine might have inadvertently caused you pain.'

I was able to reassure him I was perfectly all right. 'In fact, better than I've felt for months,' I said.

'I've been such a foolish creature, but at long last it seems I've grown up.'

The odd thing was that now we'd met each other's eyes, we couldn't look away. 'Ever since you were small,' he said, after a pause that wasn't at all awkward, 'you have held a special place in my heart. Such a sweet, sad little girl you were, and now blossomed into the loveliest young woman. I hope you realize how much you mean to me.'

My heart had begun to beat faster yet I was utterly confident. 'As do you, dear Duke, to me,' I said. 'I've always appreciated your guidance, and have thought a great deal about your advice. Especially lately.'

Another short pause. He cleared his throat. 'Does that mean you have decided to marry this person? The one you mentioned at the château?'

'No,' I said, beaming. 'It means I have decided *not* to marry him.'

I waited for him to reply but he didn't speak for a moment. Instead he suddenly threw down his napkin, pushed back his chair and got up, striding off towards the rose garden. I watched him go before coming to my senses and running after him. 'Whatever's the matter?' I asked, breathless, once I'd caught up. 'Did I say something silly?'

'Not you. Me,' he replied, looking into the distance. 'Just about to make a complete and utter fool of myself. Forgive me – must be going mad.'

Eugenie's Story

I took his hand. (Yes, even though I wasn't wearing gloves!) 'Dearest Plum,' I said, 'you're not going mad. Or if you are, then so am I. Please, tell me what you're thinking.'

Silence. I saw a muscle work in his cheek. Then, 'I was going to propose to you myself,' he said. 'Did you ever hear such a ridiculous notion?'

I gathered all the courage I possessed. Now or never: this was the defining moment of my life. 'It doesn't seem ridiculous at all,' I said. 'In fact I think it's rather a good idea. And if you *were* to ask me to marry you, I might even say yes.'

He gazed at me then, incredulous, but with such hope burning in his eyes that it brought tears of joy to my own. 'Can you really mean it?' he breathed. 'Are you sure?'

I nodded, incapable of speech, whereupon he immediately dropped to one knee and begged me to do him the honour of becoming his wife. Of course I accepted with alacrity – whereupon he took me by the waist and spun me up in the air, the two of us laughing for sheer delight. Blue sky, yellow roses, green meadows and dark cypress trees whirled about my head in a glorious kaleidoscope; by the time he had set me back down on the grass, I thought my heart would burst with happiness. He kissed me then, and that kiss wiped away the last vestige of shame, leaving me healed and whole.

As we walked back to the hotel, however, he

was already beginning to worry I might change my mind. 'You are so young and lovely,' he said. 'I am jaded, buffeted about by life. Wouldn't you prefer a husband nearer your own age?'

I assured him that was not the case. Younger men hold little appeal for me now and anyway, the Duke is only forty-one; this difference in years hardly matters when considering how ideally suited we are in every other respect. Darling Plum has all the *gravitas* I need. He is so wise and kind, and has such wonderful taste. He gives me substance. In return, I hope to bring him the energy and optimism of youth, and perhaps even children in due course, which his first wife was sadly denied. (The Duke says this misfortune, combined with an over-fondness for the roulette table, was the cause of her decline.) I am determined to be the best wife and hostess he could possibly imagine; our homes will be filled with flowers, warmth, laughter and love.

I have managed to persuade my dearest darling not to sell the Château Alma; there is a fishing lodge in Scotland and a farm in Oxfordshire that can be disposed of instead. We will spend the spring and early summer in London, and the autumn and winter in France. Plum says the château looks magical in the snow, and we can always flee to Paris should the weather become too inclement. I have such plans for the garden: box parterres, avenues of maple and hornbeam, a lake in front of the house to reflect its

Eugenie's Story

ravishing simplicity... Perhaps one day Papa might like to come and construct a wall for us around the herb garden.

I'm not sure how Mama and Papa will react when they hear of our engagement. I do so hope they will give us their blessing but even if they don't, I have decided to go ahead and marry the Duke anyway. A bold step but I am determined; I have never been more sure of anything in my life. If Mama never speaks to me again, it won't be a very great loss, and I know Papa won't abandon me. Even if he were he to cut me off without a penny (which I'm sure will not be the case), it won't matter. Plum says he would marry me with only the clothes I stand up in. He has returned to Paris to cancel the sale of the château, where we shall all shortly join him for the ordering of wedding gowns and trousseaux, before returning to England at the end of next week. I have acquired a dear little French maid, Eloise, who is coming back with me; she is so quiet and gentle and hardly needs any improvement at all.

Reading over my past escapades, I resemble nothing so much as a demented bluebottle, hurling myself repeatedly against the glass in a frantic effort to escape. Now I have become a colourful butterfly: a Peacock, perhaps, or a Red Admiral. The window has been thrown open and I am fluttering serenely through to the sun-drenched garden beyond, where a thousand beautiful flowers await.

Swallowcliffe Hall

I am going to tie this volume up with satin ribbon and hide it in a hatbox until I am too old to be wounded by the memories it contains. When we are back in London I shall order a new journal from Smythson's, bound in red Moroccan leather, in which to record the next glorious chapter of my life.

These words will be embossed in gold upon the cover:

Eugénie, Duchess of Clarebourne
Château Alma

THE END

FURTHER READING

I've come across some wonderful memoirs written by Victorian and Edwardian women in the course of my research for this book. *Seventy Years Young* by Elizabeth, Countess of Fingall, is an account of her engagement at the age of seventeen (during her first season; Eugenie would be jealous) and subsequent life with Arthur Plunkett, the eleventh Earl of Fingall. Who could resist a narrator as engaging as this?

'The grass grew higher in Meath,' she writes, 'the trees became heavier and darker, until at last I felt that the lush growth of everything was sending me asleep. It must have been in an effort to keep awake that I used to dance by myself under the beech trees those summer evenings. "I am alive," I would cry joyously. "I am alive! And no one can take that from me!"…We became so unaccustomed to the society of our fellow creatures that there was a day that summer when Fingall and I, sitting under one of the trees near the house beside the pond and seeing a carriage drive up the avenue, lay flat, hiding ourselves in the long grass that covered us, like truant children; until we saw the carriage turn from the door and drive away again, when we breathed a sigh of relief and lifted our heads.'

Consuelo Vanderbilt's autobiography, *The Glitter and the Gold*, tells the story of a less happy marriage: that of an American heiress forced by her socially ambitious mother to accept the proposal of Charles Spencer-Churchill, the ninth Duke of Marlborough. Her book gives a fascinating insight into the social and political lives of the English upper classes – as does *Life's Ebb and Flow*, by Daisy, Countess of Warwick. She was famously mistress to Bertie, the Prince of Wales and several other notable men of the time, and was given the nickname Babbling Brooke (after her husband's other title, Lord Brooke) to reflect her indiscretion about her numerous affairs.

Haply I May Remember and *Remember and Be Glad*, by Cynthia Asquith, contain marvellous accounts of country-house life and entertainment. Her mother, Lady Elcho, was a notable hostess and one of the founding 'Souls', as that group of intellectuals was known; Lady Asquith became a friend to writers such as D H Lawrence and J M Barrie, as well as a successful author in her own right. Gwen Raverat's *Period Piece* is the most charming account of an upper-middle-class Edwardian childhood in Cambridge.

Gwen was Charles Darwin's grand-daughter and her book is full of wonderful descriptions of various eccentric members of the Darwin clan.

I am also indebted to *Discretions and Indiscretions*, by Lucy, Lady Duff-Gordon, for giving such a wonderful insight into the fashions and customs of late-nineteenth-century London. Founder of the fashion house, Lucile, Lady Duff-Gordon was one of the most influential couturiers of her day, single-handedly changing the way women dressed and thought about themselves. Her own life was colourful: sister to the romantic novelist, Elinor Glyn, she survived the sinking of the *Titanic* and had booked a passage three years later on the *Lusitania*, only to cancel at the last minute because of illness. The *Lusitania* was subsequently destroyed by a German torpedo (as featured in my book, *Grace's Story*: Lord Vye dies aboard the ship in mysterious circumstances). The fictional character of Mrs Thompson in *Eugenie's Story* does not personally resemble Lucy Duff-Gordon in any way, however.

Many descriptions of the clothes and social events featured in the book are taken from issues of *The Lady* magazine of 1893, which I have been lucky enough to find in The British Library. Researching, writing and narrating this story has been a great pleasure, and if anyone enjoys it half as much, I shall be delighted.

Jennie Walters

About the Author:

Jennie Walters has had over twenty books published for children and teens, including the popular *Party Girls* series. She was partly inspired to write the 'Swallowcliffe Hall' stories by visits to beautiful old English country houses, including Kingston Lacey in Dorset, Belton House in Lincolnshire and Castle Howard in Yorkshire. When younger, she spent two years in a cliff-top boarding school converted from a Victorian mansion with wood-panelled rooms, a huge marble staircase and one of the largest collections of stuffed birds in England. Finding a silver housekeeper's châtelaine while clearing out her father-in-law's flat whetted her interest in Victorian servants and their masters and mistresses, and prompted her to create a fictional country house of her own.

Jennie lives in London with her husband and a dog, and has two grown-up sons.

For a fascinating insight into the world of English country houses and the families and servants who live in them, visit Jennie's website, packed with original photographs, historical information, extracts from servants' letters, and much more!

www.jenniewalters.com

Printed in Great Britain
by Amazon